Love is the Crooked Thing

Barbara Wersba, a former book reviewer for *The New York Times*, is an award-winning writer of books for children and teenagers. She is currently living in Sag Harbour, New York, which provides the setting for this touching and funny story, featuring Rita Formica and Arnold Bromberg.

The reader is introduced to Rita and Arnold in *Fat: A Love Story*; *Love is the Crooked Thing* continues to follow their fortunes and their story is concluded in *Beautiful Losers*.

Already published in Pan Horizons – *Fat: A Love Story*, *Tunes for a Small Harmonica* and *Crazy Vanilla*.

PAN HORIZONS

C. S. Adler
Binding Ties

Judy Blume
Forever

Bruce Brooks
The Moves Make The Man

Aidan Chambers
Dance On My Grave

Lois Duncan
The Eyes Of Karen Connors
Stranger With My Face
*I Know What You Did Last
  Summer*

Paula Fox
The Moonlight Man

Merrill Joan Gerber
I'm Kissing As Fast As I Can
*Also Known As Sadzia! The
  Belly Dancer*

Virginia Hamilton
A Little Love

Toeckey Jones
Skindeep

M. E. Kerr
*If I Love You, Am I Trapped
  Forever?*
Is That You Miss Blue?
Night Kites
Son Of Someone Famous

Norma Klein
Beginner's Love
Breaking Up
It's Not What You Expect
*It's Okay If You Don't Love
  Me*
Angel Face
Going Backwards

John Maclean
Mac

Harry Mazer
I Love You Stupid

Richard Peck
Are You In The House Alone?
Remembering The Good Times
Close Enough To Touch

Sandra Scoppettone
Long Time Between Kisses
Happy Endings Are All Alike

Jean Thesman
The Last April Dancers

Rosemary Wells
When No One Was Looking
The Man In The Woods

Barbara Wersba
Tunes For A Small Harmonica
Crazy Vanilla
Fat: A Love Story
Love Is The Crooked Thing

Patricia Windsor
The Sandman's Eyes
Killing Time

Love is the
Crooked Thing

Barbara Wersba

PAN HORIZONS

in association with **The Bodley Head**

'Brown Penny' by W. B. Yeats. Reprinted with permission
of Michael B. Yeats and Macmillan London Limited

First published in Great Britain 1987 by The Bodley Head Ltd
This Horizons edition published 1989 by Pan Books Ltd,
Cavaye Place, London SW10 9PG
in association with The Bodley Head
9 8 7 6 5 4 3 2 1
© Barbara Wersba 1987
ISBN 0 330 30731 2
Printed and bound in Great Britain by
Richard Clay Ltd, Bungay, Suffolk

LOVE IS THE CROOKED THING

1

WHEN I WAS sixteen years old, I had a love affair with a person named Arnold Bromberg. In and of itself, this might not have been unusual. I mean, sixteen-year-old people have love affairs every day. The only difference was that Arnold Bromberg was thirty-two at the time—an impractical dreamer who wrote poetry and quoted Shakespeare and played the organ. He was a large, shy, bearish sort of man who came from the Middle West and whose father was a minister. Arnold had never, in all of his thirty-two years, been able to earn a living, though he *was* writing a book on the life of Johann Sebastian Bach. He loved animals, and music, and literature, and was a terrific cook. He was also a terrific lover—but that part comes later.

Do you know what my parents did about Arnold, when they discovered that I was sleeping with him? They locked me up. Then, when it became apparent that you cannot lock an almost-grown woman in her room indefinitely, they took me to a shrink named Mrs. Perlman. They began to see Mrs. Perlman too, and pretty soon the whole family was in therapy. And for what, I ask you, for what? Simply because I had fallen in love and was sleeping with the person I loved. Simply because I was human.

I think that if I had murdered someone, they would have been calmer. Yes. Because murder, after all, is something understandable. People have been known to lose their tempers in supermarket lines and try to kill the person in front of them. Murders have been attempted on crowded New York City buses. Ordinarily, my parents are reasonable people. But they *could not understand* how I could hand over my virginity to a thirty-two-year-old loser named Arnold Bromberg. As though virginity were the Hope Diamond or something. As though it were the Holy Grail.

All of this happened in my hometown of Sag Harbor, New York, which is a place that was a whaling port in the eighteenth century and a factory town in the nineteenth century. Sag Harbor is part of something on Long Island called the Hamptons—towns near the ocean that are summer resorts—but it is the tackiest Hampton of them all, despite its motels and restaurants and antique shops. The factory that used to be its hub still stands to one side of the town like a large brick ghost, and most of us here are definitely not rich.

Take my father, who owns Tony's Auto Repair over on Clarence Street. For years he has worked like a dog just to support my mother and me, and for a long time my mother worked as a real estate sales-person to help out. My name, by the way, is Rita Formica, and I'm an only child. I also have a weight problem, an eating problem—but that too, comes later.

Oh God. Just writing all this down makes me feel like crying. Because the pressure my parents put on Arnold and me, when they discovered our affair, was so terrible that Arnold packed up his things and left. The crazy thing is that he thought they were right. "I *am* too old for you," he declared sadly, "and it isn't appropriate that we should be sleeping together. Your parents are right, my dearest. We must part."

Only Arnold Bromberg could have agreed with the enemy like that. And only Arnold Bromberg could have left me—the one person on earth he loved—behind him like wreckage on the beach. And why? Because Arnold was so good, so pure, that he never put himself first. I wanted him to fight for me, to take me and run far away to the ends of the earth. And what did he do instead? He split.

5

I had met Arnold the summer I turned sixteen, because, as usual, I needed a summer job. So when I saw an ad in the local paper that said, "Delivery-person wanted to deliver pastries for *Arnold's Cheese-cake*. No experience necessary," I answered it right away. The address was just a few blocks from my house.

The first thing that seemed odd was that the place looked like a dog grooming parlor—and the second thing that seemed odd was that it *was* a dog grooming parlor. An old, out-of-business dog grooming parlor with a cheesecake operation in the back. The person running the cheesecake business turned out to be Arnold, and at first I had no particular reaction to him except that he was a little weird. He reacted to me, though, right away. As though sunshine had come into his life. As though he had stumbled onto a million bucks.

Crazy. Here I was—five foot three and weighing two hundred pounds, dressed in an old pair of overalls and one of my father's shirts—and you would have thought that Marilyn Monroe had stepped into the room. From the moment he saw me, Arnold was in love—though it took me many weeks to realize this. The thing is, he was always paying me compliments, and asking my opinion about things, and acting like I was the most interesting person in the world. And because the cheesecake business did almost no business at all, we had plenty of time to talk. The more we talked, the more I realized what an unusual man he was—a poet and a philosopher, a brilliant musician, a person who was writing a book on Bach.

It took me a long time to realize that I was in love with Arnold Bromberg—the reason being that I had a crush on someone else at the time and was preoccupied with trying to lose weight. I was involved in the old Fat or Thin syndrome, the predicament in which you lose weight and gain weight, diet and binge, starve and gorge. And I had been caught in that predicament for most of my life—a fat person who had been fat since early childhood, and who had been through every kind of weight counseling and diet therapy known to man. I was the kind of girl you often see on the street munching something out of a bag. The kind of girl whose clothes have to be made for her because she is too large for regular apparel. The kind of girl who is the life of the party, but who is really dying inside.

If you were to ask me to give you one word—just one—that would describe my life, the word would be loneliness. Not the loneliness of the outsider—but the loneliness of someone like me, who was always popular. The minute I hit kindergarten I made sure that everyone knew who I was, and by first grade I was the resident stand-up comic of my school. But God! Do you know the kind of loneliness such a person lives with? It's the loneliness of the fourth grader who is too fat for a Halloween costume and goes trick-or-treating in her mother's orange drapes, pretending to be a pumpkin. It's the loneliness of the thirteen-year-old whose first date—a blind date—arrives at the door and says under his breath, when he sees her, "Jeez. It's Moby Dick." It's the loneliness of the person who goes to teenage parties and pretends to have a terrific time.

Which is why, when I discovered that I loved Arnold Bromberg, a kind of peace came into my soul. We had met in June, and by December we were lovers. Not that it was easy to seduce Arnold. He was so filled with scruples about my age, and my virginity, that I almost didn't get him into bed. But when we finally did make love, it was perfect. He was experienced, which—let me tell you—makes a difference. Not like fooling around with some callow teenage boy in the back of a car. Arnold was to lovemaking what sable is to fur. The best.

However. You have to realize that we only slept together from Christmas Eve till the end of January—and therefore, it was all too brief. The gentleness, the care, the thoughtfulness that Arnold put into the whole experience was over before it really began. A month. Little more than a month.

Without my mother knowing it, I went on the Pill. And, because Arnold had been helping me diet since

August, I lost forty pounds. Forty, count them, forty. Which meant that I was beginning to think about clothes and hairstyles and makeup—things I had never allowed myself to think about before. For the first time in my life, I wasn't ashamed to be naked. For the very first time I could take off my clothes in front of another person and feel beautiful.

The explosion came when my mother found my birth control pills. She went out of her mind with anger, but do you know what my father did, when she told him? He wept. I could have coped with anything—rage, hysteria, violence—but not with my father weeping. Because all of a sudden his little girl, his baby, was having sex. And it destroyed him.

Why is it that most parents cannot tolerate their kids having sex? They themselves might have lost their virginity at the age of three, but when their offspring begin to have sex, it's a threat. The subject used to come up in our family therapy sessions, the ones with Mrs. Perlman, but my father could never talk about it. His eyes would fill up with tears and he would shake his head wordlessly—letting us know how much he was suffering. His baby, his little girl, had been used for carnal purposes by some terrible man. Except, of course, that Arnold was the most sensitive, loving person in the world. No matter what we did together, he gave more than he took. Always.

At first my parents saw Mrs. Perlman on Mondays,

while I saw her on Tuesdays. Then, after rapport had been established, the three of us began to see her as a group. On Wednesdays. These were not easy sessions because, first of all, my father did not speak during them—he only wept—and second of all, my mother tended to dominate the whole thing. As shrinks go, Mrs. Perlman was not too bad. I mean, she was fair-minded and tried to give everyone equal time. *I* knew she didn't think my having sex was equal to a terrorist act in the Middle East, but of course she never said so. She was a psychiatric social worker who had trained in New York City, and she was pretty good.

Then Arnold came to one session, and disaster struck.

It was Mrs. Perlman's idea that Arnold join us, and so, after a few weeks of therapy, I brought him along to one of the Wednesday meetings. My parents knew him, of course—he had been to the house several times—but when he walked into the room with me, it was like Hitler had just entered. They went very quiet and pale, and cast sidelong looks at each other.

Teddy-bearish as always, Arnold beamed and shook hands with everyone, and smiled, and offered my father a piece of gum—which my father quickly refused. Then we all sat in a circle and Mrs. Perlman asked each of us to describe his feelings re the affair of Rita Formica and Arnold Bromberg.

My father, of course, could only weep. That was his statement to the world—bitter tears expressing agony over his daughter's downfall. By now his weeping was beginning to annoy the hell out of me, but my father was raised as a Catholic and still has all those morals. He also has a little drinking problem, and this might have been part of it. So he wept. Next, it was my mother's turn—and believe me, she didn't mince words. Arnold, she declared, was a thirty-two-year-old man who had chosen to seduce a teenage girl. "People go to jail for less," my mother announced to all of us. "It's called statutory rape."

"The laws vary from state to state," Mrs. Perlman said.

"I don't care what the laws are!" my mother said angrily. "This man has taken advantage of my child, and if I were a more vindictive person, we'd be in court right now—not in a therapy session."

"Actually . . ." I began.

"It's not your turn, Rita," said Mrs. Perlman. "Let your mother speak."

My mother glared at Arnold Bromberg. "Do you know what it's like to raise a child?" she said to him. "To sacrifice everything for a beautiful daughter, only to have her seduced by some passerby, some traveling salesman?"

"Arnold is not a traveling salesman!" I said.

"Rita, dear, let your mother speak." said Mrs. Perlman.

"Who are you, anyway?" my mother said to Arnold. "A traveling salesman, a person who's had at least ten professions and failed at all of them. Are you solvent?" she asked him furiously. "Do you earn a living? Of course not! Because let me tell you something, Mr. Bromberg, I've had you investigated. And as far as I can tell, you're nothing more than a drifter. My daughter says she wants to marry you, but it will be over my dead body. I didn't raise her to marry some kind of traveling salesman."

"He is *not* a traveling salesman," I shrieked. "For God's sake, Mother, Arnold's a writer! He's writing a book on Bach!"

My mother gave me a look that would have withered a flowering rosebush. "You don't know what you're talking about," she said. "You're still a child."

Child? I was a person who had suffered all of her life from being unloved. Oh, not by her parents, but by the world. I had suffered from the age of five with a deep, dark, existential suffering—and now, for the first time, I had found peace in the arms of a lover. This did not constitute being a child.

Surprising us all, Arnold Bromberg put out his hand, meaning that he wanted silence. I had never seen him make such a gesture—a gesture that was almost Biblical in its grandeur. He put out his hand, palm first, and my mother stopped in her tracks.

"Mrs. Formica," said Arnold, "I don't want you to say any more. Because I agree with you. I *am* too old for your daughter. And I have never earned a decent living."

My mother went pale with shock, and my father—for just a moment—stopped weeping. Mrs. Perlman also looked shocked. As for me, I was going into cardiac arrest. Metaphorically speaking.

Arnold gazed at all of us with compassion. He looked at my mother and father with compassion, at me with compassion, and even at Mrs. Perlman with compassion. "Everything you have said today is true." Arnold said to my mother. "Don't upset yourself further."

The silence in the room was so tangible you could have cut it with a knife. It was an awful silence, fraught with danger and alarm. Arnold, I thought, what are you doing? Stop, please stop, before it's too late.

"All I have to offer your daughter is love," Arnold said to my mother. "Not security, not solvency, and not even a conventional life. My interests, Mrs. Formica, have always been interests from which one cannot draw a profit. Music. Literature. Philosophy. And while I am writing a book on the life of Johann Sebastian Bach, I have no idea if it will ever be published. All I have to offer Rita is love."

"Arnold!" I cried. "You're collaborating with the enemy."

He turned his gaze on me, a sad, sweet gaze. "These people are not the enemy, Rita. They love you."

From that point onward, things went downhill. My mother, pretending she hadn't heard Arnold, kept reiterating that he was nothing more than a traveling salesman. My father got the hiccups, and Mrs. Perlman—losing authority by the second—kept telling everyone to be calm and let the other person speak. Arnold was standing by the window, mournfully smoking a cigaret. As for me, I had all the hope of a drowning man who is going under for the third time.

Within a week, Arnold Bromberg was gone. You wouldn't think that anyone could wind up his life in a week's time and disappear—but he did. After seven days of not seeing Arnold, and of missing him painfully, I arrived in front of the dog grooming parlor to see a sign that said, "For Rent" outside. Arnold was gone.

I had a key to the house, of course, and so I went inside. And it was then that my heart broke like an old piece of china breaking—because what had been our place was desolate and empty. No books in the bookcase, no sheets on the bed. Empty closets and empty shelves. Not even a houseplant remained to show that Arnold Bromberg and Rita Formica, for eight months, had known each other here.

After a few minutes, I saw the note. A small piece of paper Scotch-taped to the refrigerator. A small piece of pale-blue paper that had once been someone's stationery. A piece of paper with Arnold's handwriting on it, which said, "Into eternity, Rita. I love you."

2

INTO ETERNITY. The words were struck on my heart like an image is struck onto a coin. They followed me to school—Peterson High—and home again, and to the grocery store and the post office. Into eternity. If I could have carved the words into my flesh, I would have. But it didn't matter. They were carved into my soul.

My parents, needless to say, were overjoyed at Arnold's departure. Therapy sessions came to a halt, and thinking that objects, *things*, would make me feel better, they began to spend money on me. New clothes and new bedroom furniture, a new TV, and the promise of a motorbike. I had been begging for a motorbike for a solid year, but I didn't give a damn about it anymore.

It was March now, and there is no place as cold and blustery in March as Sag Harbor. The wind sweeps in from the east, and the skies change from charcoal to bright blue, and a sudden snowstorm can bury the town for days. In summer, our town is a playground, a resort—but March is the month when you would prefer to be somewhere else. The point is, I didn't even know it was March. Wrapped in an old coat, I walked for miles on the bay beach—the place where Arnold and I had walked so many times—and stared at the cold gray water. I thought of Arnold's love of birds, shorebirds in particular. I saw him walking beside me, hatless in the wind, his hands thrust into the pockets of his winter coat, his face uplifted to the weather. Into eternity. The words were my talisman, my magic, and I could not forget them.

One of the things that upset me was that I did not have a photograph of Arnold. I was afraid of forgetting how he looked, and so I would close my eyes and burn his image into them. A tall man with curly brown hair. Sea-green eyes. Glasses. Smooth skin and cheeks that were always ruddy. Immaculate clothes, old business suits mostly, and fingernails that were clean and filed. A green sweater, and a shaggy blue one that I particularly liked. Many pale-blue shirts, and—Arnold's trademark—sneakers. In an era of jogging shoes, Arnold Bromberg wore sneakers, even with his suits, and while at first I had found this peculiar, I later came to like it.

I went to high school every day, and talked to peo-

ple, and did my homework, and even cut a few ca-
pers—the old Rita, the clown—but I was dying inside.
And of course I had started to eat again. Sugar, potatoes, bread. A candy bar here and there, a donut
maybe. All the old bad habits returning, and me not
caring at all. Into eternity, I said to myself as I fell
asleep each night. Into eternity.

You may be wondering what my attitude toward
my parents was during these weeks. Without mincing
words, let me tell you I hated their guts. That sounds
a little strong, I know, but the fact that they were the
cause of Arnold's noble decision filled me with rage.
I had loved them before, considered them nice people,
compassionate people—and now I hated their guts.
Because of course they interpreted Arnold's departure
in their own way. "It just shows you what the guy
is really like," my father kept saying. "A little trouble,
and he takes off."

Mrs. Perlman, who I was phoning regularly, would
say, "You don't hate your parents, Rita, you're just
going through a difficult time, a time of mourning."

"What do you mean, mourning? Arnold isn't dead."

"I know dear, but he *is* gone. And you have to
allow yourself a time for grieving. If you will go
through the grief, it will pass. If you will allow your
feelings to emerge, you will be stronger later on."

"If I were braver, I'd kill myself," I said, hoping
to alarm her.

Being a therapist, Mrs. Perlman was not alarmed. "These are normal feelings," she said patiently. "Allow yourself to feel them."

And then the first postcard arrived.

I had gone to the post office that Saturday morning quite innocently, to pick up the family mail, and there it was—a rather creased little postcard from Paris, France, showing the Eiffel Tower. The message was simply this: "I love you. A.B."

Paris, France? You could have knocked me over with a feather. Kansas, I might have expected. California, even. But Arnold was in Paris.

I carried the postcard with me everywhere I went. And as it began to get soiled, I wrapped it in plastic wrap. But it was always with me, at school, at home, at the movies even. A few days later, the second postcard arrived, this one from London. "I love you," said the postcard. "A.B."

A pattern began. One postcard every few days, and always from a different city in Europe. Paris, London, Vienna, Rome. Where Arnold had gotten the money to do this kind of traveling, I did not know, but a part of me was traveling with him. Each time a postcard arrived, I would go to the local bookstore and buy a paperback on that particular city. Then I would study the city until I had some knowledge of it, traveling with Arnold in spirit. In spirit, by his side.

Soon the bookshelf by my bed was filled with paperback travel books. In my mind's eye I saw Arnold as a person in a spy movie, an old Orson Welles movie, perhaps, always on the move, wearing a raincoat and a slouch hat, checking in and out of third-rate hotels. I tried to communicate with him by closing my eyes and concentrating. I tried to find out—telepathically—if he was sleeping with anyone. No, Arnold wasn't like that. He would probably remain faithful to me for the rest of his life.

The thing that drove me crazy was that I didn't know why he was in Europe. Arnold was basically so unsophisticated he had moved to Sag Harbor simply because he liked the name "Sag Harbor." He knew nothing about the place except that he loved the ocean and seabirds, and hurricanes and ships, and so he had moved here from Kansas on the strength of the name alone. But now he was in Europe, traveling from city to city—a kind of outcast, a haunted person who still remembered me. Who loved me.

The postcards kept coming, and I continued to eat. Not just a stray candy bar here and there, not just a random donut, but food as I had known it in the old days. You see, my idea of food has always been different from other people's. Other people seem to consume meat and vegetables, dairy products and fruit, whole grains and starches—whereas my concept of food, to put it plainly, is junk. Cookies, candy, and potato chips. Pizza and strawberry shortcake. Malteds, french fries, Sara Lee cakes. Gummy Bears.

When my mother realized I was putting on weight again, she almost collapsed. She wasn't mean about it or anything, but we had been through this syndrome so many times before that she was really upset. "Oh no," she said to me, "Oh no, honey. You mustn't let this happen again. You lost forty pounds last year."

I gave her a cold, hard look and bit my tongue. Because what she had forgotten was that it was Arnold who had gotten me to lose forty pounds. Arnold Bromberg had once been fat himself, and so he knew how to help me diet. And because I had done every single thing he told me to, I had lost the weight.

But now I was alone, drifting through life like a balloon, soaring and bobbing along like a fat balloon someone had accidentally let go of. I phoned Mrs. Perlman and told her I was eating again, sneaking in and out of ice cream parlors and grocery stores like a criminal. "The terrible thing is, all I eat is junk," I said to her. "I don't eat anything normal."

Mrs. Perlman said something amazing. "Don't you think you are good enough for good food?" she said.

That one hit me hard—because it had the ring of truth to it. I ate junk food because I thought *I* was junk. I wasn't good enough for good food.

I sat there holding the phone to my ear, but saying

nothing. Because suddenly my whole life was passing before my eyes—and what I saw was a fat girl who pretended to be like everyone else, who was even the life of the party at times, but who felt as isolated as someone on a desert island. Robinson Crusoe Formica. A shipwrecked person from birth. Someone who felt so odd, so peculiar, so *wrong*, that she had never given herself any respect. It was a revelation.

"I wish I could see you in person," I said to Mrs. Perlman. "I wish we were having sessions again."

Mrs. Perlman cleared her throat, sounding slightly embarrassed. "Your parents have told me that . . ."

"I know," I said, "I know. They don't want to pay for therapy anymore. They think I'm cured. I mean, what the hell, Mrs. Perlman, they think a new TV set is the answer to my life. New bedroom furniture. A new winter coat."

"Try not to be bitter," said Mrs. Perlman.

"Right," I said. "I'll try."

As spring came to Sag Harbor—as the air became mild and the skies turned a delicate blue, and as sailboats could be seen in the harbor, tilting into the wind—something happened. I began to notice that Arnold Bromberg's postcards were coming from one place. Zurich, Switzerland. The first postcard from that city showed a narrow river with swans on it—some pretty churches in the background—and the second postcard showed a busy, rather elegant street called the Bahnhofstrasse. People milling about, shop windows, narrow blue streetcars, etc. There was a third postcard, showing some kind of modern-art museum, and then a fourth and a fifth. I rushed to the bookstore and bought a travel book on Switzerland. Zurich, said the book, is a cosmopolitan city known for banking, publishing, and churches. James Joyce is buried there. Thomas Mann lived there at one time, and also Thornton Wilder.

I have to pause to tell you something important. Which is that, at the age of sixteen, I had realized I was going to be a writer. And guess who had revealed this to me? Arnold Bromberg. We were simply talking one day, sitting in a marsh waiting for egrets to fly by—birdwatching, that is—when Arnold asked me what I wanted to do with my life, and without even thinking about it, I had said I wanted to be a writer. This was early in our relationship, but the minute the words were out, I knew they were true. Why else had I spent my life daydreaming and making up stories? Why else was I such a good liar? I couldn't look at anyone—people on the street, people in stores— without making up a scenario about them, and no matter who I met for the first time, I began to invent his life. This characteristic, Arnold told me, was the writer's characteristic. This need to rearrange the world meant that I should write fiction.

The minute I realized all this, I also realized something else. Which was that I did not want to go to college. I mean, why go to college when I could plunge right in and be an author? The minute I was sprung from that prison called Peterson High School, I intended to strike out on my own. I would live in a garret and write novels, poetry, plays. And Arnold Bromberg would be there with me, writing his book on Bach.

I had not yet told my parents about this anarchistic plan. As far as they were concerned, I was already investigating Hofstra, Stony Brook, Southampton College. As far as they knew, I was completely involved, that spring, in discussing higher education with my guidance counselor and poring over college brochures. "Rita's considering Hofstra very seriously," my mother told her friends over the phone.

Arnold Bromberg had said that a writer is the person who *writes*—every day, and for a certain number of hours. The dilettante talks about writing. The writer writes. On good days and bad days, on days when he feels well and days when he feels ill—through hangovers and the flu—the writer writes. This, said Arnold, is how you distinguish the professional from the amateur. The amateur writes when he feels like it, and does a lot of talking about inspiration. The writer sits there and pounds his typewriter. I began to read biographies of writers and saw that Arnold was correct. "It's no different than being a plumber or a carpenter," Arnold had explained. "You go to work every day and put in your hours."

But what had I written thus far? Twenty-three poems and a rather odd play about a woman who drinks herself to death in Vienna. Half of a novel I didn't understand myself. Masses of love letters, unmailed, to Arnold Bromberg.

"Putting words together is fairly easy," Arnold had said to me. "Constructing the whole thing, however, is a different matter."

Oh Arnold, you were so right. Because I wrote furiously that spring, putting in my hours—even purchasing a new typewriter—only to wind up stuck, stymied, blocked. I had always been an *A* student in English, but this was different. Constructing a novel was tough.

My novel was called *Rosamund*—the symbolism being that she was a rose of the world, something beautiful, yet something doomed to fade—and I myself had trouble figuring it out. The plot was complicated. There were, perhaps, too many characters.

Rosamund is about a girl who has religious visions, sort of like Bernadette of Lourdes. Everyone in her French village thinks she is crazy, and to make life even more difficult, she is tremendously beautiful. She wants only to live a religious life, and heal the sick, but this terrible beauty she has keeps throwing her in the path of men. Her twin brother, Robert, who lives in Greece, has been separated from her since birth, but he is determined to find her. Robert is married to a woman named Nicole, and Nicole, in turn, has a few secrets of her own—namely, an early marriage to a man from whom she was never divorced. At the end of the book I intended to have Robert—who has gone blind—arrive in Rosamund's village, to be cured by her. Her fame as a healer is widespread by now, and she is much older—at least forty. Drawn to each other in a mystical way, Rosamund and Robert sleep together. When they discover that they are brother and sister, they commit suicide by walking into the sea.

Anyway. It was lucky that I was the member of our family whose job it was to get the mail at the post office every day. Because the postcards that said, "I love you. A.B." were coming thick and fast. And all of them from Zurich. By the end of April I was obsessed with Zurich and was beginning to haunt secondhand bookstores, looking for volumes on that topic. There were very few, but the ones that I did locate showed me a lovely old city that was built on the banks of a river, a city that had a lot of ancient churches and winding streets, a city that could have stepped out of the Middle Ages.

Arnold, I said mentally, what are you doing in Zurich? What has drawn you there? Is it because the place is intellectual, because they have museums and

25

art galleries? Is it the libraries and the bookstores? Why are you there, Arnold, and why are your postcards so cryptic? Why send me dozens of postcards if you want to break up with me? Most people, when they break up, do not send postcards from Switzerland.

Suddenly it hit me. The reason Arnold Bromberg was sending me so many postcards was that he wanted me to join him. In Zurich. Three thousand miles away.

3

I WAS SURE of it. Beneath the cryptic words "I love you. A.B." was a cry from the heart, a cry from Arnold asking me to run away from the small town of Sag Harbor and become a citizen of the world. With a rush of excitement, I saw myself on a wide-bodied jet, speeding across the Atlantic. I saw myself landing at some glamorous airport and taking a glamorous taxi into the city of Zurich. The trouble was . . . I did not know where Arnold was staying. Damn! The only things his postcards showed were churches and shops, the River Limmat, and some stained-glass windows by Chagall. There were postcards showing university buildings, and postcards of an opera house, and many postcards of swans. But no hotel.

26

I was stumped. But only momentarily. Because I felt that if I could just *get* to Zurich, then maybe I could find him. Hire a detective, go to the police. The German teacher at Peterson High, Mrs. Schneider, had told me that in Zurich they spoke a dialect called Swiss-German, but that everything printed was in real German. I signed up for a German class on the spot, as an auditor, surprising Mrs. Schneider greatly. But I was determined now, and you have no idea what I am like when I make up my mind about something.

I went to a travel agent in East Hampton and learned—with a shock—that a round-trip ticket to Zurich cost eight hundred dollars. "There's a reduction in the fare if you stay for three weeks," the agent said to me. "How long were you planning on staying?"

"A weekend," I replied. And as a look of astonishment crossed her face, I made a speedy exit.

Who would have thought that it cost eight hundred dollars to go to Europe? Eight hundred was almost a thousand—and in my savings account there was exactly thirty-five dollars. It would be possible to escape my vigilant parents for one weekend by telling them I was visiting a friend in New York City, Corry Brown. And in the space of one weekend I could talk to Arnold and work out our future.

I went to bed that night—after I had seen the travel agent—with my mind buzzing like a hive full of bees.

Eight hundred dollars, I thought, eight hundred dollars. Add a few bucks to it for taxis and food, and you are up to a thousand. And how does a sixteen-year-old person acquire one thousand dollars, tell me that, I said into the darkness.

Sell my body on the streets of Sag Harbor? No, not even funny. Rob a bank? Hock my new television set and also the new bedroom furniture? Nope, too obvious. Steal my mother's diamond engagement ring, which she never wears anymore, and hock that? No, too ignominious, too crummy. Eight hundred dollars, said my mind. With food and taxis, make it a thousand. What a pity you have no special talent, no special genius that could earn you a fast buck. . . .

At two A.M. I woke up with a start, as though I had had an electric shock. Because I knew how to get the money.

4

AT A QUARTER TO twelve the following Saturday, I was walking up Main Street toward the house of a person named Doris Morris. My appointment with Miss Morris was for twelve o'clock noon, and I was determined to be on time. Doris Morris was a local

woman who had made good as a writer of
romances—and then she had become an agent,
worked out of her house, a large Victorian mansion,
and she was a big success. Local newspapers did fea-
ture stories on the success of Doris Morris. Radio
stations interviewed her.

Until a few years ago Doris Morris had simply been
the lady who worked at the local dry-cleaning store,
the person to whom one handed dirty slacks and
sweaters over the counter, the person who would say,
"I'm sorry, kid. They couldn't get that spot out. What
was it, gravy or something?" Tall and a little weird-
looking, with dyed black hair, she was a fixture in
one's life—the lady who worked at the dry cleaner's.
Then, all of a sudden, Doris wasn't working there
anymore. Doris was writing something called historical romance under the name of Amanda Starcross.
Doris was making money. And no sooner had she
made her first fortune than she bought a house on
Main Street and turned herself into an agent. She still
wrote some of the Amanda Starcross books, to keep
her hand in the business, but now most of the books
were written by other people. Doris had a "stable"
of writers, people who turned out romances and westerns and detective stories. And everyone in town knew
about this—including me.

I had under my arm that day the first twenty pages
of *Rosamund*, which I intended to have Miss Morris

hat the hell—it was worth a try. I
perienced, and I knew that my chances
Miss Morris were a million to one,
to try. Writing a book for Miss Morris
way I knew to make any dough.

I rang the doorbell of the big white Victorian house
and waited. After a long time, a maid—yes, a maid
in uniform—answered and ushered me into the living
room. I was really amazed by the house, because it
was very elaborate. Victorian furniture. Beautiful rugs
on the floor. A grand piano.

Upstairs, I could hear typewriters clacking away—
and lining the bookshelves of the living room were
yards and yards of paperbacks. I was just reaching for
one when Miss Morris came into the room.

I had planned not to recognize her. I mean, not to
recognize her as the lady from the dry-cleaning store.
Such recognition could only embarrass us both and
get us off on the wrong foot. But the minute Miss
Morris came into the room, she grinned at me. "The
blue overalls," she said. "The fuzzy pink sweater."

I laughed. "Well, yes. Hello there, Miss Morris.
It's nice to see you again."

She had changed. I mean, she was still tall and
weird-looking, with dyed black hair, but now she
wore expensive slacks, and a frilly white blouse, and
high heels. Lots of jewelry and makeup. A big diamond ring on one hand. She looked glamorous. And
very very successful.

"Sit down," she said. "Take a load off."

I sat down in a big Victorian chair.

"A cup of tea?" she asked.

I shook my head, feeling a little uncomfortable. "It was nice of you to give me an appointment," I said.

"Hell," she said, "why not? My secretary said you sounded desperate. And anyway, I remembered you from the old days."

"The blue overalls? The fuzzy pink sweater?"

"Right, right, I remembered your name. So what's the problem? You want to write books for me?"

Numbly, I nodded. Because the whole thing was beginning to seem ridiculous. "I . . . I brought you a sample of my work," I said to her. "Twenty pages of a novel. I mean, I haven't published anything yet, and I'm only a junior in high school, but I do want to be a writer. Truly."

Miss Morris frowned. "You know the kind of books we turn out here?"

"Uh, yes. I think so."

"You ever read any historical romance? Any westerns?"

"Well . . ."

"I thought not. But that's no problem. If you work hard, you can learn the form. I've got housewives working for me, and businessmen, and college students. All kinds of people. What you have to realize is, this stuff isn't T. S. Eliot. This stuff is a product."

"Right," I said.

"What we turn out here is a product," said Doris Morris. "A product like cornflakes or vitamin-B enriched white bread. T. S. Eliot we are not."

"I understand."

Miss Morris looked dubious. "Maybe you do and maybe you don't. You look like the kind who writes poetry or something."

I blushed. "Well . . ."

"I knew it," she sighed. "A teenage poet. Well, poets we are not. T.S. Eliot we are not."

"I need money very badly. It's an emergency."

Miss Morris gazed at me for a moment. "OK, so hand over those twenty pages. I'll read them in the den."

Trembling a little, I gave her the first chapter of *Rosamund*, and she disappeared down the hallway. Left alone in the living room, I walked over to the bookshelves again and studied their contents. Yards and yards of paperbacks, all in bright colors. I took one from the shelf. It was called *Savage Eden*, and the cover showed a man and a woman with their clothes partly off, embracing. "She hated him for making her crave his touch!" said the front cover. On the back, it said, "Flaming Rose, the Indian maiden, didn't know what would become of her if her captor tired of her. But until then, she was a slave to his desires, a slave to ecstasy!" I had seen these kinds of books in supermarkets and drugstores for years, but had never really looked at one. God! I thought. What am I getting into?

There were around twenty Amanda Starcross books that had the word "savage" in their titles. *Love With a Savage*, *Savage Thunder*, *Savage Encounter*, *Dark Savage Sky*. Etc. And on every one of them, the cover showed two half-naked people cleaving to each other, if that is the right word. The people were always partly undressed, and in the background were scenes of Southern plantations and pirate ships. Another group of paperbacks was written by someone named Charlotte DuLac. These all had the word "song" in their titles. *Windsong*, *Nightsong*, *Lovesong*, *Starsong*. I opened one of these in the middle and read the following: "His steely eyes raked her full young breasts. And in her imagination she could feel his lips there—breaking every law known to God and Man!"

Miss Morris returned and sank down into one of the big Victorian chairs. "I like what you've written," she said. "It's nutty, but I like it. But religion is not our subject here. These books—because I can't see you doing westerns or anything—these Starcross books deal with erotic romance. The kind that doesn't really exist, but the kind that every woman wants. So what you do, kid, is you take a dozen of these home and study them. And if you think you can write one, you give me a call. *I* create the plots, and my partner,

33

Suzy, does the historical research for you. All you do is write."

"Ah, could I ask you what . . ."

"We pay three thousand bucks per book," said Doris Morris, "and the contract is a simple one. There are no royalties, but when you get experience, you should be able to turn one of these out in a month. Also," she said, "our secretaries, the girls who type your manuscript, do not use computers. Computers, word processors, I am definitely against."

"Why?"

"Because they emit radiation—and I'm very much into health. When you come here, you don't smoke. OK? And you don't drink coffee. You have a little herb tea or nothing. A few rice cakes, maybe."

"I see."

"We work through three publishers," Doris Morris continued, "and the publisher that does the romances is called Gazelle Books. What you'll learn, when you've read a lot of these, is that basically they're all the same story. Early in the book, the girl—who is always a headstrong type—loses her virginity to some gorgeous, mysterious, slightly cruel man. By the end of the book she has *tamed* this man and he has come to adore her. But first there's got to be a lot of complication and misunderstanding, the hero estranged from the heroine, and she estranged from him, and so on. Sometimes, a second man comes into the picture—a type who is noble but dull—and often there's a second woman too, as a contrast to the heroine. The sex has got to be erotic without being porn. Get it?"

I didn't get it at all, but I nodded my head—and soon Miss Morris was piling my arms with historical romances. "Here are the Starcross books," she said. "Go home, study them, and give me a call." She looked me up and down. "Haven't you lost some weight this year? Didn't you use to be heavier?"

"Uh, yes," I said.

Miss Morris chuckled. "The blue overalls. The fuzzy pink sweater."

Loaded down with Amanda Starcross books, I staggered home. The more I thought about it, the less likely it seemed that I could ever write in this field. Pirates and Indian slave girls. Mail-order brides going west.

That week, ignoring almost everything else, I began to read my way through the romances. They were terribly long—four hundred pages each—and so badly written that I kept shuddering as I read. But Miss Morris was right—they were all the same story. Placed in England in the eighteenth century, or the American West in the nineteenth century, with backgrounds of old Southern houses or pirate enclaves in Barbados, all the stories dealt with virgins who got raped/seduced by gorgeous, mysterious men. The women

35

have ash-blond or raven hair, are breathtakingly beautiful, and the men make love like they have just been through a course with Masters and Johnson. Cruel heroes are tamed. Weak heroines turn out to have guts. There is a lot of wish fulfillment and many descriptions of clothes. People's eyes are always tarnished silver or cornflower blue. Sex is described symphonically. I mean, violins and flutes play when people have orgasms. White doves, metaphorically speaking, are released into the air.

I felt very conflicted. Because, being in love myself, I felt I knew something about passion. But my passion for Arnold Bromberg was *nothing* like the things that went on in these books. Arnold, I thought, why are you in Zurich when I need you so much? What are you doing there?

After six days of reading one book a day, I began to think about the situation more practically. Was three thousand dollars good pay? It seemed like a lot of money to me, and it would definitely get me to Zurich, but was it enough for writing a whole book? In view of the fact that Miss Morris wrote the plots, and her partner did the research, maybe it was. I was going to spring for it. A recent atheist, but now a believer—because Arnold was—I began to pray at night, just before I fell asleep. "God," I said silently, "I know you don't like bargains, but please give me the ability to write a historical romance. If you will just let me write one, I'll stop eating junk. I mean it, God. This is a promise."

5

I HAD PHONED Miss Morris and said that I would write a romance for her. "Fine," she said. "I'll whip up a plot for you. But first, write a sample chapter, something off the top of your head. Let me see what you can do."

Those words sent me into a panic, but then, calming down a little, I decided to get organized. The first thing to do was to copy down a typical paragraph, an archetype, if you will, of the romance style. Something I could use as a model.

Elvira felt shame scorch her face as the golden coins cascaded into her hands. She was nothing but a doxy now, a wench of the Caribbean. As she thought of the rough men who would use her, she almost fainted. And as she thought of Percival, waiting for her back in England, she stifled a sob. The once-proper dress she had worn was now ripped to shreds, exposing her ample breasts. Two feet away, the pirate king leered. In his flashing eyes she saw her present and her

37

future. Yes, she was nothing but a doxy now, a luscious object made for the use of men.

I read the paragraph—taken from *Savage Encounter* —over a few times and sighed. Would I ever be able to write this way? I, who had written twenty-three poems and the most beautiful, unmailed, love letters in the world? It didn't seem likely, but I was going to try.

Neglecting my homework completely, I began to invent a sample chapter for Miss Morris. It was all about an innocent English girl named Dabney Cavendish, who is crossing the ocean to join her fiancé in the colonies when she is kidnapped by a pirate named Jason Hardtower. Relying heavily on the plot of *Savage Encounter*, I had Dabney raped/seduced by Jason Hardtower—only to discover that her fiancé, Rye Randolph, is a captive on board. And he has seen the entire rape because he has escaped his bonds and is hiding in the pirate's private cupboard. Dabney, of course, is mortified by what has happened, but secretly pleased. The sex with Hardtower has been all violins and flutes.

A few days after my interview with Doris Morris, I walked up the steps to her house with my sample chapter in hand. It was neatly typed, it was in a manila folder, but whether it was any good or not, I had not the slightest idea.

The maid ushered me into the living room and I waited. From upstairs came the sound of typewriters. From the kitchen, somewhere in the rear of the house, came a delicious smell of cooking. As usual these days, hunger overwhelmed me. During the months I had been dieting, with Arnold by my side, I had known very little hunger. Now I was starved. For sugar and potatoes and bread. For muffins and strawberry ice cream. For french fries and malts, cheeseburgers and butterscotch sundaes. For Gummy Bears. With a sense of horror, I saw myself gaining back the forty pounds I had lost. I saw myself returning to my Fat Clothes. Overalls and raincoats. Boots. My father's shirts.

There was a full-length mirror in Miss Morris' living room, so I stepped over to it and stared at myself. What I saw was a person five foot three who was plump but not obese. Who was even sort of pretty. I was wearing jeans and a pink shirt, my hair was tied back with a ribbon, the way Arnold used to like it, and I had on some pale-pink lipstick. I would always be short, of course, too short, but I did not have to be fat. Don't blow it! said Rita Formica, you've only gained back ten pounds and you can lose them again. Darling, said Amanda Starcross, think of Arnold, your lover, waiting for you in Switzerland.

Miss Morris appeared, gave me a grin and a wink, and disappeared down the hallway with my sample chapter. In fifteen minutes she was back, looking elegant in black slacks and a satin blouse, gold bracelets jangling from her wrists. "So," she said. "Let's talk."

We sat down facing each other, and because I had recently taken up smoking as a way to avoid eating, I yearned for a cigaret. But Miss Morris had said she disapproved of them. She looked at me, and I looked at her—as nervous as if I were about to open on Broadway. I almost felt sick.

"You look pale," Miss Morris said. "You want a cup of tea or something?"

I shook my head, feeling sicker by the moment. Because I was sure that she hadn't liked my chapter. Almost positive.

"OK," she said, "so let's get down to business. I read the chapter and I liked it. You've caught on to the form pretty well. But honey, really! Your writing isn't sexy enough. In fact, it isn't sexy at all."

"It isn't?" I said weakly.

"Take the scene where your pirate rapes the girl, Dabney. It's like your characters are disembodied or something. Like they have no private parts."

"But you said no porn."

"Right, no porn. But the words *do* have to be sexy. Now I know you are only—what is it, sixteen, seventeen?—so maybe you can't do what I want."

Crazy, I thought. I have just been through a passionate love affair with Arnold, and she says that I can't describe sex.

40

"Look," I said, "I really want to do this. So will you let me try again? I'm sure I'll get it after a few tries."

Miss Morris frowned and walked over to the bookcase, where she extracted a romance by Charlotte DuLac. She opened the book at random. "Now listen to this," she instructed. " 'She let him remove her clothes and sighed rapturously as his naked form came down upon her own. And there in his arms, her blood sang with the ancient singing of her tribe and her breasts swelled with passion. She no longer resisted him, and no longer feared his power. Pulling him closer, she felt her body meld with his, felt his need for her rising and tumbling like the great wave they had lived through in the storm. In unison, they reached their goal and cried aloud. In unison, they collapsed back into a starry silence.' "

"God," I said involuntarily. "That's terrible."

Miss Morris nodded. "You're damn right it's terrible. But it's the *genre*, kid, it's the *genre*. And either you learn to do it, or you don't."

"Could I ask you something?"

"Sure. Fire away."

"Why do all these women have to get raped? I mean, it's part seduction, but it is also rape. How come?"

"A woman's fantasy is to lose control with someone who cares for her. You know what I mean? If a dame is overpowered, she doesn't have to take responsibility for her feelings. Sex without guilt, it's called. Men, of course, do not have that problem."

I was amazed by these words, but also impressed. Doris Morris had obviously done a lot of thinking about all this. "Will you give me another chance?" I asked. "With a little practice, I think I can do it."

"Sure," she said, as she walked me to the door, "why not? We go through writers here the way other people go through Kleenex. The burnout is amazing."

I wanted to ask what she meant by that, but I didn't have a chance, because a man came through the front door. A young man who was dressed in tight Levi's, cowboy boots, and a checked shirt. He had thick black hair and wore sunglasses. He was very handsome. "Good morning, ladies," he said.

"Good morning, Jerry," said Miss Morris. "How are you?"

The person named Jerry was looking me over. I mean, looking me over from head to toe. It made me nervous. "Jerry, this is Rita Formica," said Miss Morris. "She may be working for us."

"Charmed," said Jerry.

"Hi," I said.

"Rita, this is Jerry Malone," Miss Morris continued. "He writes westerns for us under the name of Victor Colorado."

"Victor Colorado?" I said.

"That's right," said Jerry amiably. "Victor Colorado."

42

I wanted to laugh, but didn't. "What kind of westerns?"

He smiled at me, revealing a mouthful of perfect white teeth. "The Wrangler series. You know. *The Wrangler and the Lady*, *The Wrangler Goes East*, *The Wrangler in Love*."

"Oh," I said, "sure. I've read them." Because what did it hurt to lie?

Jerry took off his sunglasses and smiled at me again. He was even more handsome than I thought, dashing even. But I did not like him. We had only been standing in the doorway for about three minutes, but I knew that I did not like this person. He was some kind of an operator.

"I hope I'll be seeing you again," Jerry said to me.

"Right," I replied. "So long now."

"Do your homework!" Doris Morris called after me, as I headed down the path. "And then give me a call."

6

VICTOR COLORADO. It was a phony name for a phony person, I decided. Nevertheless, I went off to the dime store that afternoon and bought three of his books. They were simply western versions of the Amanda

Starcross stories. Set on the ranches and prairies of nineteenth-century America, the stories were about girls who got raped/seduced in covered wagons instead of pirate ships. Instead of English lords, the men were wranglers, ropers, and wagon chiefs. Many of the ravished maidens were half-breed Indian girls with names like Dawn Flower. The difference was that these books were more explicit about sex. The sex scenes, as a matter of fact, made me blush.

I stayed up till three the next morning, rewriting my sample chapter for Miss Morris—and dozed all the way through English class, French class, and Algebra III. The writing of romances was going to ruin my high school career, but what the hell. I would recover next year, when I would be a senior.

That evening I was locked in my room again, working on the rape of Dabney Cavendish by Jason Hardtower, when the phone in the hall rang. My mother answered it and knocked on my door. "It's for you," she said. "A man."

I hurried out into the hall—grateful to see that Mom had gone back to the living room to watch television. She was trying to be good these days, about not prying into my personal life. But then, what personal life did I have? One postcard every few days from Switzerland. Sharp, painful memories of a man named Arnold Bromberg.

"Rita?" said a smooth voice on the phone. "It's Jerry speaking."

44

"Who?"

"Jerry Malone. Or Victor Colorado. Whichever you prefer."

I was very surprised. "Oh. Hi there."

"Doris' secretary gave me your phone number. I hope you don't mind."

"Well . . ." I said dubiously.

"The reason I'm calling is that I'd like to ask you out tomorrow night. There's a good film playing over in East Hampton. I thought you might like to go."

Well, let me tell you. I was stunned. Because—phony or not—this Jerry was a very handsome guy. For a moment I was tempted, but then I came to my senses and said, "That's very nice of you, Victor. I mean, Jerry. But I don't go out these days. I'm engaged."

He didn't skip a beat—that's how smooth he was. "Not even to a film? Not even for a cup of coffee?"

"Nope. I don't date anymore. Sorry."

"Who's the lucky fellow?"

"He's traveling in Europe at the moment. You wouldn't know him."

There was a sigh on the other end of the phone. "Well, that's a real disappointment, Rita. I don't know many people in town, and I would have enjoyed your company."

"How come?" I asked. "How come you don't know anyone?"

"I've been here for only a year, and most of that

time I've been writing the Colorado books. There are several of us who write them, of course, but I've worked so hard that I haven't made any friends. I'm from the coast, actually."

"California?"

"Right, L.A. My real profession is acting. I'm only writing the westerns to support myself."

"What have you acted in?" I asked.

He chuckled. "You name it, I've done it. Soaps, sitcoms, a few series. I was on *Mickey and Mike* for two years. Do you ever watch it?"

"The one about the two cops? Yeah, I do. My parents watch it all the time."

"I came east because I was fed up with television. It's Broadway I'm after."

"Well," I said. Because that was all I could think of saying.

"I'll let you go now," said Jerry. "But I'm sorry I won't be seeing you. I would have enjoyed it."

I hung up the phone with a strange sense of loss. His phoniness was due to him being an actor—and now that I understood that, I didn't dislike him so much.

A few days later, I handed in my revised sample chapter to Miss Morris. I had worked hard to make it lurid—but Miss Morris was still dubious. "It's awfully pure," she said, "awfully noble. You hardly got their clothes off." When tears of disappointment came to my eyes, she suddenly changed her mind. "Hell," she said, "you'll catch on to it eventually." And with that, she handed me the outline of my first Amanda Starcross book.

I took the outline, along with many pages of historical research and a whole sheaf of "romance guidelines," and went home as excited as if I had just won the Pulitzer Prize. My book was called *Savage Sunset* and it was placed in the time of the Civil War. The characters were called Temple Shannon and Chance Darby, Tawny O'Rourke and Royal Blane. Miss Morris' notes to me said the book should be at least four hundred pages long, with chapters of twenty to thirty pages each. Wow, I thought. This is not going to be easy.

By now it was May, and the weather was so gorgeous that I found myself missing Arnold with a feeling that was close to despair. As yachts and sailboats began to moor in the harbor, as the summer restaurants began to open again, as swans flew over the bay beach—and as it became warm enough to sunbathe— I thought of him constantly. These were our beaches and our swans, and this sapphire bay, stretching out as far as the eye could see, was our landscape. We had met in early June, in weather just like this, and in a few weeks it would be June again. The characters in my book, *Savage Sunset*, might heave and pant, gasp and swoon, but with Arnold and me it was different.

A look from him—just one look—was enough to commit me for a lifetime. The gentlest kiss was my undoing. No two people on earth were ever more right for each other—and Arnold's unconventionality, or whatever you want to call it, was at the heart of the whole thing. I had never liked ordinary men, in fact they tended to turn me off. Whereas Arnold was so shy, so subtle, so . . . restrained, that I found him thrilling. Because underneath his shyness was a volcano.

I kept his postcards in a special box, one I hid in the closet, and every night I would take the postcards out and spread them on my desk. The rooftops of Zurich, covered with snow. An ancient square with a fountain in it. And always, pictures of swans on the River Limmat. "I love you," said the postcards. "A.B." I would gaze at the postcards and go back to my work on *Savage Sunset*. And every time a good sentence came to me, out of context or not, I would write it down. "An evil smile quirked the corners of his mouth," I wrote. "Her soft eyes reminded him of warm brandy."

My mother, of course, thought that I was locked in my room every night doing homework. "I've never seen her study this way," she told her friend Edith over the telephone. "It's wonderful."

Wonderful? I was sleeping through all of my morning classes, making at least one of my teachers, Mr.

48

Vacarro, think that I was doing drugs. Quite bluntly, he asked me about this, putting it right on the line. "My God, Mr. Vacarro, no!" I'd said to him. "I'm not into anything like that. I just have, uh, insomnia. I don't sleep well at night."

"I'll make an appointment for you with Miss Stapleton," he said kindly. "Maybe she can help." Miss Stapleton was the school psychologist.

"No," I said, "please don't do that. I'll be better in a few weeks. Really."

One night when I was alone in the house—my parents having gone to a movie—Corry phoned. Corry Brown, from New York City. Corry, who had run up such a phone bill talking to me that her mother had forbidden her to call me anymore. I, in turn, had been forbidden to phone *her*—our phone bills having reached the hundreds of dollars. But now, in May, it was Corry on the other end of the phone and I was glad. Corry was an ex-Sag Harborite who had moved to the city. Until a year ago, we had been bosom friends.

"I miss you," she said. "It's hell here. I wish we hadn't moved."

"You don't like Miss Spencer's?" I asked. Corry was going to private school these days. It made a difference.

"Like it?" she said. "If I were a more violent person, I'd bomb the place. They have *tea dances* every month, can you believe it? And boys from military schools come and dance with us."

"God," I said.

"Here I am, living in an age of space travel and rock videos, living in an age where everyone turns on, and we're having tea dances. With plates of little cookies. With cups of tea."

"Are you going out with anyone? Is anything happening?"

"Happening? What could happen to *me*? The most exciting thing that's happened all year is that I fell down in Bloomingdale's and broke my front tooth. It cost a thousand dollars to fix it."

All of a sudden, I knew it was time to tell Corry about my plans for going to Europe. Corry had never met Arnold, but she knew about him. Our conversations about Arnold, as a matter of fact, were the reason the phone bills had been so high.

I plunged in and told her everything. About the postcards that kept coming from Zurich, and about my job with Miss Morris. At that news, she groaned. "Oh no," she said, "not *romances*."

"What's wrong with romances? They're only a product. They don't mean anything."

"Are you kidding? Those crappy books are completely antifeminist. They're putting the movement back a hundred years."

"Oh, come on," I said. "They're not that bad."

"My mother reads them," Corry said flatly, "and I think they're rotting her mind."

"I'm going to be paid three thousand bucks. For one book."

Suddenly, Corry became practical. "Do they give you royalties?" she asked.

"Uh, no. Actually not."

"What about subsidiary rights?"

"What kind of rights?"

"Subsidiary. You know—movies, television."

I have forgotten to mention that Corry's father is a lawyer, and that she plans on being a lawyer too. It gives her a certain practicality.

"I don't know what you mean," I said.

"What I mean is this: Do you get any money if one of your books gets turned into a movie?"

"I don't think so."

"Well, that stinks. It's exploitive."

"Look Corry, I only want to write one book, so I can go to Zurich. For the weekend."

She giggled. "That's going to be one hell of an expensive weekend. And what do you think you'll accomplish there?"

"I don't know. I just know that I have to see Arnold. Talk to him, make love with him. I *miss* him so much, Corry, it's awful."

"You're too sentimental," she said. "You always have been."

51

"But I'm in love!"

"Rita, look. Even my father doesn't go to Europe for the weekend—and he goes all the time."

"I am going for a weekend," I said firmly. "Probably, toward the end of summer. And I want you to cover for me."

"OK," she said, "so you're going to Europe for the weekend. But at least make it the Labor Day weekend. It's longer."

7

I HAD BEEN working on *Savage Sunset* for ten days and was getting absolutely nowhere. To begin with, the plot Miss Morris had devised for me was so complicated I couldn't keep it in my mind. It kept unraveling and rolling away, like a ball of yarn. Roughly, the plot was about hot-blooded Temple Shannon, a northerner born in the South, who is desperate to get behind Rebel lines, enemy lines, so she can find her missing brother. Dressed as a boy, Temple steals into the White House one night and has an interview with President Lincoln—yes, President Lincoln—who arranges for her to get behind enemy lines if she will do some spying for him. Meanwhile, somewhere early in the book, Temple is raped/seduced by the gorgeous Chance Darby, who seems to be an aide of Lincoln's but is really a spy himself, for the South. Temple's guide through enemy lines will be a noble but dull person named Royal Blane, who wants Temple, but who has been told by Chance that she is nothing but a whore. Then there is Tawny O'Rourke, a *real* whore, but with a heart of gold, who saves Temple by impersonating her at a critical moment when Temple has been captured by Rebel soldiers.

Ten days. Ten days of writing pages and tearing them up. Of not sleeping at night. Of sleeping, instead, through all my morning classes. English, French, Algebra III. Ten days of smoking instead of eating sugar. Of smoking too much, and soothing myself with candy. Ten days of breaking my bargain with God.

One morning there was a note in my mailbox, at the post office, from Miss Morris. It requested me to come over to her house and sign my contract. I phoned Miss Morris' secretary and said I would be there at four o'clock, right after school. And let me tell you, I was very nervous. Because I was signing a contract for something that I was afraid I couldn't do.

Miss Morris, as usual, was cheerful and kind—her gold bracelets jangling, her cheeks highly rouged. I read the contract, understood not a word of it, and signed it. "Is there anything about, uh, subsidiary

53

rights in this contract?" I asked meekly. "I mean, movies, and things like that."

Miss Morris gave me a cool look. "No subsidiary rights. Take it or leave it."

I took it, and bid Miss Morris good-bye. And I was just walking down the path to the street when I bumped into Jerry. He had a manuscript under his arm, and once again was wearing Levis, boots, and dark glasses. He looked just as handsome as before.

"Well," he said. "What luck."

"Luck?" I repeated foolishly. Because I was very glad to see him. Don't ask me why.

He took off his sunglasses and smiled at me. That radiant smile. Those perfect teeth. "I've been thinking about you for days—and here you are. What luck."

"I've been busy writing," I said. "I got the job."

"Wonderful," he breathed. "You'll do it well. I'm sure of that."

"I don't know," I replied. "I'm having an awful lot of trouble. I mean, my book takes place during the Civil War, and the plot is incredible. And the details! What people wore, what kind of food they ate, what kind of carriages they rode in. It's overwhelming."

Jerry reached out and brushed a strand of hair away from my eyes. It made me shudder a little. "Would you like some help?" he asked. "I'm an old hand at this. In fact, I write some of the Charlotte DuLac books, in my spare time."

"Well . . ."

"I know—you're engaged and you don't go out with people. So let's just call it a business meeting, all right? I'll help you with the book, and you'll give me the pleasure of your company."

I looked at Jerry Malone, alias Victor Colorado, and instead of saying something cool and sophisticated, I said, "Why do you wear cowboy clothes?"

He smiled. "It gets me in the mood. To write westerns."

"So what do you wear when you're writing romances? A dress?"

He didn't think this was funny. "Look, sweetheart, do you want to go out with me or not? I can't keep asking you."

"Right," I said hastily. "Sure, I'll come. I mean, if it's just business. Where shall we go?"

"Let's make it The Cooper Hotel. Tomorrow evening at six."

I was very surprised. Because the restaurant at The Cooper Hotel, in Sag Harbor, is one of the most expensive in the Hamptons. "That would be nice," I said.

He smiled again, that movie-star smile. "Look gorgeous for me, OK?"

I laughed nervously. "Sure."

"Wear blue. It's my favorite color."

"Right," I said, "you've got it. So long now, Victor. I mean, Jerry."

"I'll be thinking of you till tomorrow night," he said.

8

I MUST ADMIT that I worked on myself the next afternoon. Curling my hair, ironing my one good blue dress, polishing a pair of black leather pumps. Borrowing some earrings from my mother. Choosing a new shade of lipstick. I was going out to dinner with a boy from school, I told my parents. And they, thinking that Arnold Bromberg was a thing of the past, smiled approvingly. "Bring your fella home after dinner," my father suggested. "We'd like to meet him." Stammering a little, I said I didn't know whether or not that would be possible. My date had a sprained ankle and couldn't walk far. We were simply going to meet at a restaurant and have dinner.

This is a business meeting, I told myself as I ran a bubble bath that afternoon. Strictly business, I murmured as I took the curlers out of my hair. Jerry will help me with the book, I recited as I put on a dab of my mother's Chanel No. 5. It's nothing personal.

The Cooper Hotel isn't far from my house, so at a quarter to six I started out on foot. The blue dress had been bought months ago, when I was thinner, and now it was straining at the seams. I was more used to jogging shoes than high heels, and so I was staggering a little. My mother's earrings hurt my ears.

I passed a shop window on Main Street and took a look at myself. The effect wasn't bad, but it wasn't really me. It was some kind of creation. A lady author, off to have dinner with an actor friend.

Jerry was waiting for me in the lobby of the hotel—and this time he was dressed in tight black western pants, a shirt and a string tie, and black boots with a high polish on them. I looked at the boots, thought of Arnold's sneakers, and felt my heart sink. What was I doing here? How could I be so disloyal? It's only dinner, said my inner voice, the voice of Rita Formica. You little fool, said Amanda Starcross, the man is gorgeous! Why not have a good time?

Jerry bent and kissed me swiftly, on the cheek. "Good evening," he said.

"Good evening," I said. "Good evening."

"How lovely you look. And you *did* wear blue."

"Sure," I replied. "Why not?"

The hostess ushered us to a small table in the atrium, which is a long gallery with a glass roof. The restaurant at The Cooper Hotel is made up of three rooms in different styles—and of all of them, the atrium is the best. I had my sixteenth-birthday party there.

"Is this table all right?" Jerry asked me. "Quiet enough?"

"Oh, yes," I replied. "Certainly."

He took off his dark glasses and smiled at me. "Good, good." Then he opened the menu. "Aha. They have Blanquette de Veau tonight."

In my mind's eye, I saw a blanket with some gravy on it. I banished the image and watched Jerry across the table.

"May I see a wine list?" Jerry said to the waiter. And the waiter brought it at once.

"Actually," I said to Jerry, "I don't drink very much. Hardly at all."

"It doesn't matter, sweetheart. I'm going to order a bottle of Chablis for myself. You can have a sip of mine."

On our table was one flickering candle, and a rose in a vase. "Do you mind if I smoke?" Jerry asked.

I shook my head, feeling more uncomfortable by the moment. Arnold, I thought, what am I doing here?

The waiter brought the bottle of wine to our table, uncorked it, and poured a small amount into Jerry's glass. He tasted it, thought for a moment, and nodded. "Excellent," he said.

After we had placed our order—the Blanquette de Veau and an endive salad—Jerry poured himself some wine and raised his glass to me. "Here's looking at *you*, sweetheart."

Here's looking at *you*. . . . It had a familiar ring, but I didn't know why.

"It's time for you to tell me your life story." Jerry said.

"You first," I answered, taking a sip of his wine.

Jerry Malone, it turned out, was an actor from Los Angeles who had been writing westerns for years. Twelve months ago he had come to Long Island with an acting company that played at Guild Hall, in East Hampton, and when the show had closed, he had stayed on. He drove into New York once a week, to see his agent, and spent the rest of the time writing westerns and swimming up at Gurney's Inn, which is a resort in Montauk. He had been acting since he was twelve years old.

"And how old are you now?" I asked him.

"Twenty-six. And yourself?"

"Eighteen," I lied. "I'll be nineteen in June."

The Blanquette de Veau arrived, and we ate it in silence. Jerry glanced at me and said, "Everything all right, sweetheart?"

"Oh, yes. Sure."

He reached across the table and stroked my cheek for a moment. "Good."

My appreciation of the Blanquette de Veau had been spoiled by my thinking of it as a winter blanket covered with gravy. And I didn't think the salad was too great either. But when it came to dessert, I saw that there was strawberry shortcake on the menu, and I brightened up.

"You haven't told me *your* life story," Jerry said, as our desserts arrived.

"Another time," I said. "What I'd really like to talk about is my book."

He glanced quickly at me. "Why don't we go over to my place and work on it? I don't live far from here."

"Oh, no. I don't think that will be necessary. I mean, why don't we talk about it right here? Over coffee?"

"It would be more comfortable at my place."

"I'd prefer to stay here."

He laughed. "All right, sweetheart. We'll have our coffee in the lobby—and work on your book."

Ordering two brandies and two coffees, Jerry led me into the lobby and sank down on one of the large leather couches. I handed him the fifteen pages of *Savage Sunset* I had brought with me, and he read them—groaning as he read.

"That bad?" I asked.

"Well . . ." he said, finishing the last page, "it isn't that it's bad. I mean, you've caught on to the form and all that. But you've done the first fifteen pages without a hint of sex. Why should the reader read on?"

"I don't know. Beats me."

"The trick is to have the first sexual encounter almost at once. For example—suppose Temple breaks into the White House by shinnying up a vine or something, jumps into a room on the third floor, which she thinks is the President's but which really belongs to Chance Darby. She crawls in the window, he apprehends her, there's a struggle . . . and then he realizes that she's a girl. Her hat falls off and her luxurious hair tumbles about her shoulders. He feels her breasts. It's dark, neither can really see the other, but he's gotten horny. And so he takes her."

"Just like that?"

"Yes, just like that."

"I just can't believe she could shinny up a vine at the White House. Where are the guards?"

"Drunk," said Jerry. "Asleep. There's been a party."

"How do you shinny up a vine?"

He shrugged. "Does it matter?"

A half hour later we were walking along the wharf, where there are shops and restaurants, and where the big yachts tie up in summer. There was a full moon and it was casting a silver path across the water. In the distance we could see the lights of Shelter Island.

Jerry had his arm around my shoulders as we walked, and though I didn't want his arm there, I wasn't sure what to do about it. He had made it so clear he wanted to make out with me that I was confused. Because the question was, *why?*

We paused at the end of the wharf and stared out at the water. Jerry's grip on my shoulder tightened—

61

and then I felt his lips brush my hair. "You're lovely," he said. "Do you know that?"

By now you are probably aware of the fact that I am not a person who ordinarily feels lovely. For most of my life—with the exception of Arnold—I have felt like the following with men: a klutz, a fool, a blimp, a fatty, an oddball, a freak. You name it, I've felt it. But "lovely" I have rarely felt. So I was flattered.

"I think I should go home now," I said to Jerry. "It's late."

"May I walk you there?"

"No, no. It's just a few blocks."

"I insist," he said.

We walked the four blocks to my house, on Madison Street, but I stopped before we reached the front yard. I didn't want my parents to see us. Jerry bent down and kissed my cheek. "I like you so much," he said. "You're such a lovely girl."

"Jerry," I said, "how *do* you shinny up a vine?"

9

"ZURICH," said the travel book, "is an enchanting city. We can find its medieval past in the Old Town—a treasure of stately houses with beautiful windows, oriels, and lucarnes. Here the antique sellers have their shops and galleries, and here the craftsmen ply their wares. Steep alleys intertwine like veins in a hand. On dreamlike squares, framed by high façades, you can hear the bubbling of fountains. A combination of the old and the new, set like a jewel on the River Limmat, Zurich stands alone—unique among the cities of Europe."

I put down the book and sighed. No wonder Arnold had settled in Zurich. It sounded wonderful, glamorous, exciting. And here I was, sitting in a small town on the end of Long Island, trying to write a dirty book. Because—after another phone conversation with Corry—I had decided that romances were definitely salacious. "I can't get enough sex into my prose," I had complained to Corry. "There must be something wrong with me."

"There's nothing wrong with you," she said. "You just can't do porn, that's all."

"Porn? These books aren't porn. Miss Morris said no porn."

"It's soft porn," Corry explained. "Marshmallow porn, if you want to call it that. But it's written to arouse."

"I guess you think porn is antifeminist," I said wearily.

"*Think?* I know it is! Look, I've read those idiot books, and the women in them are victims. They never have any choice. Men force them into sex and make slaves of them."

"Then why do people *read* them?" I yelled.

"Because they're the opiate of the housewife!" she yelled back.

"So what's wrong with opiates?" I shouted. But Corry had hung up.

Two minutes after that happened, the phone rang again and it was Victor Colorado on the line. The bogus cowboy. "Sweetheart?" said the smooth voice. "How are you tonight?"

"Fine," I said. "Perfect."

"I just wanted to tell you what a great time I had with you the other night."

"Me too," I lied. "It was wonderful."

I braced myself—certain he was about to ask me out again, and certain I would refuse. Despite his good looks, I did not intend to start dating Victor Colorado.

"I just wanted to tell you that I'm going into the city for a few days," he said. "I'm up for a part in the new Betty Bacall play."

"The new what?"

"The new Lauren Bacall play," he explained patiently. "Lauren's real name is Betty."

"Oh. Well. That's nice."

"I didn't want you to call me and find no one home."

"Right," I replied.

"Stay beautiful for me, will you? I'll be back in the Hamptons soon."

Quite inappropriately, I laughed. "What's funny?" he asked.

"Nothing," I said. "Nothing at all."

I hung up the phone thinking of Jerry's cowboy boots—and then I thought of Arnold's beautiful white sneakers. "What's the matter with this guy?" my father had asked me once. "Can't he afford shoes?"

Useless to explain to my parents that Arnold was what the French call *un original*—someone different and unique, someone who stands out from other people—and useless to explain that this was why I loved him. Recalling how briefly we had been lovers, I felt a lump come into my throat. Christmas Eve until the end of January.

Why was Jerry Malone interested in me? That was the question. Jerry Malone was so good-looking he could have had any woman in the world. In the city, there were probably dozens of women who would make out with him, women who didn't need to be taken to expensive restaurants and wooed on moonlit wharfs. Mature women, his own age. Actresses.

My mind veered back to Arnold again, remembering a snowy afternoon in January when we had made love. The town had been hushed under falling snow—only the sound of a train in the distance—and we had been lost in each other for a long long time. Finally, Arnold sat up in bed and lit a cigaret. "I love you," he said.

65

"Why?" I asked. It was the first time I had ever asked such a thing, and he was surprised.

"Why?" he echoed.

"Yes. Why do you love me? You've never said."

He blew a stream of smoke into the air, and then, abruptly, he put the cigaret out. "I love you because we are the same person," he said. "Two sides of a single coin."

Tears—sudden, unexpected—came into my eyes, and I looked at this large man who was my lover and knew that I would never understand him. I was a part of him, but did not understand him, and that was very strange.

"Do you think people are meant for each other?" I asked. "Like in old movies, old plays?"

He smiled and pulled me close to him. "Yes, darling. I do."

We sank back on the pillows, holding each other close. "Then *we* must be meant for each other," I said. "Don't you think so?"

"I do."

"Two sides of a single coin. That's very deep."

"Shh," Arnold whispered. "Go to sleep."

"In the middle of the day?"

"Why not?"

"I'm not sleepy. . . . Why don't you recite something for me. A poem."

"I can't think of anything right now."

I kissed him. "Yes, you can, Arnold. Concentrate."

"Ezra Pound?" he suggested. "Yeats?"

"Yeats," I agreed. "What was the name of that woman he loved? The Irish patriot?"

"Maud Gonne."

"Right. You told me about her once."

Arnold propped himself up on the pillows and stared into space. "The poem is called 'Brown Penny,' and he wrote it around 1910. I don't think you know it."

"I love the way you always sound like an English teacher. It makes me laugh."

"Do you want to hear it or not?"

"Yes. I do."

"Then be a good girl and listen."

> I whispered, 'I am too young,'
> And then, 'I am old enough';
> Wherefore I threw a penny
> To find out if I might love.
> 'Go and love, go and love, young man,
> If the lady be young and fair.'
> Ah, penny, brown penny, brown penny,
> I am looped in the loops of her hair.
> O love is the crooked thing,
> There is nobody wise enough
> To find out all that is in it,
> For he would be thinking of love
> Till the stars had run away
> And the shadows eaten the moon.
> Ah, penny, brown penny, brown penny,
> One cannot begin it too soon.

Then there was only silence and the two of us holding each other. Silence, with the snow falling outside and the whistle of a train in the distance. Silence, enveloping us protectively, our arms around each other, our lips touching lightly. Silence, only silence. Because all of the words had been said.

10

"TEMPLE STRUGGLED vainly," I wrote, "but Chance Darby was too strong for her, too muscular. Tearing the hat from her head, he cried aloud with surprise as he realized that she was a woman. Then he ripped open her shirt. 'Aha!' he cried, 'I thought so all along. We deal harshly with female spies here in the White House, my pretty! Now, tell me your mission.' "

I groaned, ripped the page out of the typewriter, inserted a new piece of paper, and began again.

"Temple was terrified," I wrote, "and she struggled like a wildcat, but the man, Chance Darby, was too strong for her. Tearing the hat from her head, he saw that she was, indeed, a woman. Then he felt for the two protuberances that he expected might be under her shirt. 'Aha!' he cried. 'I thought so! Do you know what happens to female spies who try to enter the White House, my pretty one? Do you know their fate?' "

Oh, God. It kept getting worse instead of better. I simply could not write the scene where Temple tries to see President Lincoln—which meant that I still had not gotten beyond page fifteen. It was early June, school was out, I had been writing for days—but the whole thing just kept getting worse. Not only was I blocked in writing about sex, but the more I worked, the more I realized that Arnold had been right. *Constructing* the thing was the hard part. Not just the words, but the armature.

I was running into problems that I hadn't even known existed in writing. Such as the fact that my events either happened all at once—or over the space of ten pages. Vital things would occur in one sentence, whereas stupid things, like women getting dressed, would take forever. How did you get people from one room into another? How did you avoid the monotonous "he said, she said" syndrome?

Then there was the research—the pages and pages of historical stuff compiled by Miss Morris' partner. What kind of underclothes the women wore, what kind of pistols were used in dueling, what the beds were like, how people took baths. I had phoned Miss Morris to ask if the historical part had to be perfect, and she said, yes, it did. "We're just like Hollywood," she said to me. "We get the background right."

Yes, and ruin everything else, I wanted to say. But of course I didn't.

I phoned Corry one afternoon, when my father was at the auto shop and my mother was grocery shopping, and asked for help. "I'm getting absolutely nowhere," I said, "and I'm scared. I mean, what if I can't do this?"

"You'll do it, you'll do it," she said grimly. "Whether it is *worth* doing is another thing."

"How's Ronald?" I asked. Ronald Studebaker was someone Corry had just met—a student at Columbia University.

"How's Ronald?" she said. "Ronald is boring. All he talks about is fossils."

"How come?"

"He's going to be a paleontologist, that's how come. So he's very much into fossils. He even gave me one, as a present. It looks like a turd."

"Well, at least he takes you out."

"Right, right. To the Museum of Natural History. To look at fossils."

"I . . . I've met someone too," I said tentatively. "But he's strange, and I don't really like him."

Corry's ears seemed to prick up. "No kidding? You haven't mentioned any new person to me. What's happening?"

70

"If you'll just slow down, I'll tell you about it."

But what was there to tell? I hadn't been out with Jerry Malone since the night at The Cooper Hotel, but I must say, he was still trying. Little notes in my box at the post office, saying, "Hi there, beautiful. Have a good day," and a bunch of flowers left on my doorstep with a note, and at least two or three phone calls a week. All of which aroused my mother's interest no end.

I am engaged, I would tell him, and don't go out with anyone. You're a hard woman, he would reply. Yes, I'd say, I am.

I told Corry the whole tale, about meeting Jerry at Miss Morris' house and about going to dinner with him. "He came on very strong when we stood on the wharf in the moonlight," I said. "It was upsetting."

"You mean because of Arnold?"

"Yes. I felt unfaithful."

"Rita," said Corry patiently, "has it ever occurred to you that Arnold might have found a girl in Zurich? That he might be making out with someone this very moment?"

I felt a chill go through my body. It was a ridiculous thought, an improbable thought, but ice ran through me all the same. "Impossible," I said.

"No, it is not impossible, because men are like that. Any port in a storm, so to speak. I mean, did he promise you to be faithful? Did you ever talk about it?"

"Of course we didn't. He left town without any warning."

"Arnold is a male, a virile male, and he may be making out with some Swiss person. That doesn't mean he doesn't love you, it just means he's making out. So I don't see why you shouldn't date this cowboy if you want to."

"But I *don't* want to date him."

"Well, think about it," she said. "We better hang up now, because of the phone bill. Did yours come yet?"

"No. Did yours?"

"Alas, no. And believe me, I'm nervous about it."

"Should we write letters instead?"

"No, come into town. Or I'll come out there or something."

"OK, Corry. Good-bye."

I hung up the phone with a sinking feeling in my stomach—because what Corry didn't know was that Arnold had once been in love with a ballet dancer named Rose. Not that Arnold had ever been promiscuous. He had, in fact, had only two affairs before me—but the last one was with Rose. When I had asked him about her, he had told me she was in Europe, touring with a ballet company. And now Arnold was in Europe too.

I went into my room, locked the door, and began to pace the floor. I could see how Arnold could fall in love with a ballet dancer, the esthetic quality of the whole thing overwhelming him. And I could see how he might respect Rose for being dedicated to her art. I could even see *Rose*—thin, lovely, attenuated, pale—and the more this apparition came before me, the sicker I felt. Arnold was a very sexual person. Rose was in Europe. Arnold had wanted to marry Rose, and had once followed her all the way to New York City from Kansas. Did Zurich have a special theater for ballet companies? I dragged out one of my travel books and learned that Zurich was very well known for ballet. Traveling companies appeared at the Zurich opera house all the time.

11

"'SIR,' SAID TEMPLE to President Lincoln, 'I have come here on a mission of life or death. It concerns my brother.' The President, clad only in his bathrobe, sighed, sat down in an easy chair, and lit his pipe. 'Go on, little lady, I'm listening.'

"It had not been easy for Temple Shannon to get into the White House. The struggle with Chance Darby, and the subsequent rape, had been a terrible price to pay. She knew how she must look to President

Lincoln—her hair a mess, her clothes ripped by Chance's greedy hands—but nonetheless she persisted. 'I need to get behind enemy lines,' she said. 'Rebel lines. My brother's life is at stake.'

"'Now, now, little lady,' said the President. 'It can't be as bad as that. Why don't you have a drink with me? I'll ring for the maid.'"

"*Shit!*" I said, tearing the page out of the typewriter. It was wrong, wrong, wrong. To begin with, President Lincoln probably didn't drink. And he wouldn't have had a maid, he would have had a valet. And I couldn't picture him sitting there in his bathrobe. I had reached page twenty-five now, but it had taken weeks to do this, and I was exhausted. I even dreamed about President Lincoln and Temple Shannon at night, but always in the wrong setting. In one dream they had been walking through the Museum of Natural History, admiring fossils.

I can't do this, I said to myself, it's impossible, I can't do this, and I'll never get to Zurich. As visions of Arnold and Rose came before me, I stifled a sob. I saw them walking by the River Limmat, feeding swans. I saw them making love in some small, obscure hotel.

I went into my bathroom and turned on the tub. A hot bath helped me think—and I needed to consider whether I could write this book at all, whether I would have to ask Miss Morris to release me from my contract. Was such a thing possible? Could you get released? I poured in some bubble bath and sank down into the comforting water. "Everything OK?" my mother called through the door.

"Of course!" I said. "I'm just taking a bath."

Just for the record here, let me say that I was no longer feeling so antagonistic toward my parents. Time had taken away much of my anger toward them—and, these days, my mother was being solicitous about me because I had told her I was writing a novel. A summer project for English class. A privilege given only to *A* students, of course. Had she known that on page five of this novel a girl dressed as a boy gets raped on the third floor of the White House, she would not have been so pleased.

I sank lower into the water, letting the bubbles swirl around my chin. Arnold's postcards were not coming as frequently now, and it frightened me. I closed my eyes and tried to concentrate. If I couldn't write the book, then maybe I could pay someone to do it for me, one of Miss Morris' hack writers. Out of my three thousand bucks I could give my proxy one thousand. Or we could collaborate.

I sat straight up in the tub, splashing water over the side. Jerry Malone, of course! Jerry, who wanted to make out with me. Jerry, alias Victor, who was an old pro at the writing of romances. But what would make him want to write an entire book for me? Not money, because he seemed to be earning plenty of that. And not fame, because he wasn't even a real writer. Not money, not fame, but . . . sex.

Even though I was sitting in a hot bath, I felt myself go cold. What a terrible idea! And yet in one of the Starcross books, *Savage Lightning*, a woman named Melanie Maidcastle had given herself to a man she hated, Brennan Moore, in order to save her true love, Gilbert. Playing for time while Gilbert escaped his enemies, Melanie had made slow sensuous love with the villainous Brennan—sacrificing herself, yet remaining pure in her heart.

Was it such a bad idea? I, whom very few men found attractive, turned Victor Colorado on. And the *reason* I turned him on—I was beginning to suspect— was because I was hard to get. I could tease him, of course, get him to write the book while procrastinating, but that was a crummy thing to do. I didn't believe in teasing. Would Victor write a book simply out of admiration for me? Bitterly, I laughed aloud. It would be a cold day in hell before he'd do that.

Arnold, I thought, tell me what to do. Would it break your heart if I made love with someone else? Are you, at this very moment, making love with Rose? Where did the morality of the whole thing lie? If making out with Victor got me to Zurich, then it couldn't be wrong. Because by being faithful to Arnold I could remain on Long Island for the rest of my life.

I stood up, wrapped a bath towel around me, and went into my room—where I took out a book called *Zurich, Past and Present*. Such beautiful pictures. The city lit up at night. Artists sketching on a stone embankment. Outdoor cafes in summer, narrow blue streetcars on the Bahnhofstrasse, a magnificent place called St. Peter's Square, and the towers of the Grossmunster cathedral rising against a leaden sky.

What would Temple Shannon do in such a predicament? I asked myself. And the answer came right away. Temple would do whatever was necessary to be with the man she loved.

12

"IT'S SUCH A beautiful night," I said to Victor Colorado, alias Jerry Malone. "I love the month of June."

"Me too," he whispered into my hair.

We were standing on the end of the wharf, once again looking at the lights of Shelter Island, and Jerry had his arms around me. It was unfortunate, but I thought I was going to throw up—either the result of the duckling with orange sauce we had had at the restaurant, or the result of Jerry. All I need to do, I thought bitterly, is be sick. *That* will end the whole thing.

"Would you like to go back to my place?" he asked. "We could listen to some music."

"Sure," I said. "But let's just stand here for a moment. It's such a beautiful night."

He continued to nibble at my hair, while my mind raced. Jerry Malone had been so thrilled when I phoned and invited myself out with him that I was stunned. *Why* did he like me so much? Once again, we had met at an expensive restaurant—The Captain's Table—and once again he had ordered the best things on the menu. But duckling with orange sauce was definitely not my thing, and now I felt queasy. Jerry, on the other hand, was very turned on. I had worn the blue dress for him and curled my hair. And now he was nibbling it.

His lips moved from my hair to my cheek—from my cheek to my neck, and I felt sicker than ever. I needed to be near a john, in case I threw up. "Let's go to your place," I said. "It's chilly out here."

Jerry was wearing his tight black western pants, and his boots, but this time he had on a rather extravagant pink shirt, made of some shiny material, with broad lapels. It was awful, and reminded me of old pirate movies with Errol Flynn. The kind my mother watches on television.

"God, you turn me on," Jerry whispered into my hair.

We walked the two blocks to his apartment in silence, Jerry obviously very aroused—and me feeling like I was going to the guillotine. I wondered if he had any Pepto-Bismol in his house, any Tums.

Well, let me tell you. His apartment was a shock. I mean, in view of the restaurants we had been going to, and his general style, I had thought that he would live in some very posh place—a condo overlooking the harbor. But do you know where he lived? In a one-room apartment over the health food store, on Main Street. And the only things in the apartment were a water bed, a stereo, a card table, and his clothes. My mind reeled. A water bed and a stereo. Heaps of clothes on the floor. What did it mean?

The minute we were inside the door, he kissed me and ran his hands up and down my body. "I'm crazy about you," he said.

"Do you have any club soda?" I asked. "I have just the tiniest bit of indigestion."

He looked like a balloon that has been pricked by a pin. "Club soda?"

"Yeah, club soda. It settles the stomach."

Shaking his head a little, Jerry went into the pullman-type kitchen and poured two glasses of club soda.

"Here you are," he said. "Your wish is my command."

There was only one chair in the room, a deep sling chair, so I sank down into it. Jerry sat on the water bed. Raising his glass to me, he said, "Here's looking at *you*, sweetheart."

Suddenly I knew where the words came from. From *Casablanca*. Only what Humphrey Bogart had said to Ingrid Bergman was "Here's looking at *you*, kid."

In the time that it took to sip the club soda, I studied Jerry—trying to decide whether or not I could make out with him. Most women would find him gorgeous—that lean body, that thick black hair—but to me, he was like some kind of third-rate movie star. He probably washed his hair with Vidal Sassoon shampoo. He probably wore men's cologne. "Feeling better?" he asked hopefully. God, I thought, he looks like a fox who is about to devour a rabbit.

"Not yet," I said. "Do you have any more club soda?"

Looking at me a little oddly, Jerry went back to the kitchen for another bottle of club soda. "Have you lived here long?" I asked politely.

He sat down on the water bed again. "Not long. It's just a place to crash. I have a bigger apartment in the city." All of a sudden, his eyes lit up. "Would you like to smoke a joint? I have some very beautiful stuff."

"No, no," I replied. "I mean, thank you all the same, but I don't smoke grass."

"It settles the stomach," he said with a grin. "Everyone says so."

The club soda hadn't helped my indigestion. In fact, I was beginning to feel worse. "Do you have a bathroom here?" I inquired.

"Of course. Why?"

"No reason," I said nervously.

"Sweetheart—come over here and sit down. You're much too far away."

Sitting down on the water bed was like sitting down on a small ocean covered with plastic. The water kept sloshing back and forth under us. I tried to imagine making love with someone on such a surface, and couldn't.

"Jerry . . ." I said, as his arm slid around my waist, as once again his lips nibbled my hair. "I have a favor to ask you."

"You name it, you've got it," he said, nibbling my neck.

"It's a very *big* favor. I don't know if you'll want to do it."

"For you, sweetheart, anything," he whispered. "Anything at all."

I was having trouble keeping my balance on the water bed. And the waves sloshing around underneath us made me think of my unsettled stomach. Dear God, I thought, please don't let me puke.

"It's the biggest favor I've ever asked anyone," I murmured.

His hand cupped my breast. "Anything, sweetheart, anything."

I pulled away from him and looked him straight in the eye. "Would you write my book for me? *Savage Sunset?*"

To my astonishment, he laughed. "What's so funny?" I asked.

"I don't know," he said. "I guess I expected you to say something else. You want me to write your *book?*"

"Yes. My book."

His hand was still holding my breast. Like it was a melon he was about to buy at the grocery store. "And what'll you give me if I do write it?" he asked.

"Me. On the water bed."

Oddly enough, he seemed shocked. "That's a pretty cold-blooded way of saying it."

"Well, I'm sorry, Jerry. But if you'll write my book for me, I'll be glad to sleep with you. And I'll also give you half the money."

He rose to his feet and walked over to the window. "That's a real turnoff. You know?"

"How do you mean?"

"Well, it's like you're selling yourself to me or something."

"Exactly," I said. My stomach was starting to churn again. It worried me.

Jerry looked angry. "What's so important about this book? Why do you need money so badly?"

"To get to Europe. My fiancé is there."

He struck his forehead with his fist. It seemed like an overly theatrical gesture, but what the hell. He was an actor. "God," he said, "what a turnoff."

"Why?"

"*Why*? Oh sweetheart, you really are naive. Are you a virgin or something? Don't you know anything?"

"I am not a virgin," I announced, "and I know a great deal about life. But at the moment, I am about to throw up. Could you tell me, please, where the bathroom is?"

Two minutes later I was locked in his bathroom, being sick. When I emerged again, he was sitting in the sling chair reading a newspaper. "Feeling better?" he asked coldly.

"Yes," I said. "Much."

"Perhaps you'd like a cup of tea," he said in an even colder voice.

"Actually," I said. "I would."

So we had tea together, and when I felt stronger we discussed my book. I told him the problems I was having with Temple and President Lincoln, and he told me that these problems could be easily solved. "How many pages have you done?" he asked me.

"Twenty-five," I replied. "And it's taken me weeks to do that much."

"This is the damndest situation I've ever been in. I mean, it's bizarre. I write a book for you, and you sleep with me."

"Right," I said. "Barter."

"And this is supposed to turn me on? This exchange of services?"

"Sure. Why not?"

"Do you know how weird you are?" he asked. "I mean, do you *know*?"

"I never said I was normal," I said with dignity. "But then, who is?"

A few minutes later, Jerry walked me out to the hallway. It was interesting, I thought, that he hadn't offered to take me home. Things were definitely on a different footing now.

"I like to sleep late," he said, "so don't phone me in the morning. Just slip the pages you've done under my door, along with the outline. I'll start working on the book tomorrow night."

"Gee. That's wonderful."

"I won't take half the money, but I will take a third. Because I can probably write the book in a few weeks."

"Thank you. And whenever you would like to go to bed with me, please let me know."

"Oh, I will, I will," he said. "It sounds thrilling."

"Jerry? Did you get the part in the Betty Bacall play? The one you went to New York about."

"There was no Betty Bacall play," he said coldly. "I only said that to impress you."

"God," I said. "I don't understand anything anymore."

"Neither do I," he replied. "Life is a labyrinth."

13

LIFE IS A labyrinth, I murmured to myself the next day, as I sat in the Heavenly Cafe on Main Street, eating a hot-fudge sundae. Truer words had never been spoken. And how amazing that Jerry had told the truth about the Lauren Bacall play. Yes, we were definitely on a different footing now, and it felt fine. I would go to bed with Jerry like someone doing a day's work. A plumber or a carpenter.

I took a spoonful of the hot-fudge sundae, complete with nuts, cherry, and whipped cream—and felt the old guilt wash over me, the guilt I always felt when eating junk. But what could I do? It was either eat sweets or smoke myself to death, and sweets, at least, did not give you cancer. Since Arnold had disappeared, in February, I had gained fifteen pounds.

I glanced across the restaurant and, to my horror, saw Doris Morris sitting in a booth drinking a cup of tea. At the same moment that I saw her, she saw me and waved. "Hi there!" she called.

The one person in the world I did not wish to see at that moment was Doris Morris. But there was nothing I could do about it. She was already heading for my table, the cup of tea in her hand. "Well, hello there," she said. "Mind if I sit down?"

"Uh, no, Miss Morris, of course not. It's nice to see you."

She sat down opposite me, dressed attractively, if flamboyantly, in red slacks and a yellow blouse. Lots of jewelry and makeup. That very black hair. "How's the book coming along?" she asked. "I haven't heard from you lately."

"Fine," I said quickly, "everything is coming along fine. I . . . I've just been working so hard that I haven't had time to phone."

"Any problems? Any stumbling blocks?"

"No, no, everything is fine. I'll be finished in a few weeks."

"Good," she said, taking a sip of her tea. Then she noticed the sundae I was eating. "Off the diet, huh?"

"I haven't really been *on* a diet. I should be, though."

"Hell," she said, "enjoy yourself while you can. Life is short."

Suddenly I felt curious about Doris Morris. About her life, and her background, and how she had gotten into the romance business. "Could I ask you something?" I said. "Something personal?"

She winked at me. "Sure, kid. Fire away."

"How did you go from . . . I mean, how did . . ."

"How did I go from rags to riches?" she said. "Is that what you're asking?"

"Well, yes. In a way."

"My life story is what you want?"

"Yes, I'm curious. I mean, if you don't mind."

"Hell," she said, "I don't mind. I'm an open book, no secrets at all. I guess you're asking because you want to be a full-fledged writer now. And writers are curious people."

"True."

"It's simple. I got myself involved with Scientific Religion, the think-positive movement, and then everything fell into my lap." Noticing the surprise on my face, Miss Morris grinned. "You never heard of Scientific Religion? Well, it's a wonderful movement, based entirely on positive thinking and positive belief. Positive belief is the core of the whole thing. *Think* successful, and you will *be* successful. That's their motto, and it works."

"But how did you . . ."

"How did I get started? By accident, except that of course there are no accidents. You see, I was a gypsy in my youth. In New York."

I had an image of Miss Morris in Gypsy clothes, riding in a caravan down Fifth Avenue. She had gold loops in her ears and a rose between her teeth. "A Gypsy?"

"I don't mean a *Gypsy* gypsy. I mean a gypsy in the theater, a chorus girl. All the chorus kids are called gypsies."

"Oh," I said. "I see."

"Around twenty years ago I was dancing up a storm on the old White Way. You ever hear of a show called *Serendipity*?"

"Well, no. Actually not."

"That's OK. It was before your time. But *Serendipity* was a very big hit. Played at the Winter Garden for two years, and I was one of the gypsies in it. I even went on one night for the second lead, when she got food poisoning from something she ate in a Mexican restaurant. Anyway, I was a gypsy. You name the show, I was in it. Musicals, mostly, though I did a couple of straight plays too. It's a tough life, you know, not for the faint of heart, but I was pretty successful."

"Then why did you come to Sag Harbor? I mean, if you were so successful in New York."

"Hold your horses, kid, I'm getting to that part.

My downfall was a man named Everett Emberley. I met him backstage one night and I was gone. I mean, *gone*."

"You fell in love with him?" I asked timidly. Because I was surprised at the things Miss Morris was telling me. Surprised at her openness.

"Fell in love doesn't describe it. I was *gone*. And Everett Emberley lived in Sag Harbor on a yacht. Winter and summer. So I followed him down here and we set up housekeeping on the boat. But of course he was a bum, like all of the guys I've been involved with, a real bum. So what was there for me to do when the relationship ended, years later? When Everett sailed away?"

"Work at the dry-cleaning store?"

"You've got it. Work at the dry-cleaning store. By then, of course, I was too old for hoofing and I had lost all my connections—the agents and so forth. Betrayed by Everett Emberley, right? It would make a good title for a book. But hell, I was in my late thirties by then, and you can't be a gypsy forever. They only want young kids for the chorus, pretty kids. So I went to work at the dry cleaner's and worked there for many years. Feeling sorry for myself. Drinking too much. Screwing around."

Miss Morris paused to take a sip of tea, and I sat there dumbfounded. Her frankness was amazing.

"*Then,*" she continued, "something interesting

happened. A girl friend of mine gives me a book on Scientific Religion, the think-positive movement, and the minute I read it, I'm hooked. *Think* successful and you will *be* successful, says the book. Think successful, and you can do anything in the world. The book is written by someone called Dr. Merry Whiteacre, and she has a Sunday-morning show on television, a real rouser, so I start watching the show. And I get hooked on the whole philosophy. Not that I'm an idealist. I just don't want to spend my old age in a dry-cleaning store. So I start practicing Scientific Religion. And when my girl friend, Rachel, asks me one day, quite casually, what I would like to do more than anything else in the world, I say back to her, 'I'd like to write one of those romances you're always reading, Rachel. I'd like to make a few bucks.' "

Out of breath for the moment, Miss Morris paused and took another sip of her tea. "Am I boring the pants off you?"

"No, no. I find all this very fascinating."

"Fascinating, I'm not sure about. But it *is* rags to riches. 'Yep,' I say to Rachel, 'I want to write one of those potboilers you take to bed with you every night, and get rich.' And by God, that's just what I did."

I was hanging on to Miss Morris' every word. "But wasn't it hard at first? The technique and everything?"

"Of course it was hard! What isn't hard in the beginning? You think life is a featherbed, a bowl of cherries? Everything is hard. But after a few months, I get the hang of the whole thing, and the very first book I write is published. I give myself the name Amanda Starcross, write a few more, and suddenly the dough is rolling in. Well hell, it doesn't take me long to realize that if one book makes money, then a dozen books could make more. So I turn myself into an agent, get myself a stable of writers—Rachel is one of them, by the way—and go into business. And that's the story."

"Wow," I said. I had meant to say something more sophisticated, but it was "wow" that came out.

"So now you know all my secrets," said Miss Morris. "You can put my life in a book. Disguised, of course."

A few minutes later we were standing out on the sidewalk. "Keep pounding the old typewriter," Miss Morris said. "Because I want to see a few chapters soon."

"Absolutely," I replied, shaking hands with her.

"By the way. My secretary told me, a few weeks ago, that Jerry had asked for your phone number. Is he bothering you or something?"

"Oh no," I said quickly. "Not at all. We've just had dinner together a few times."

Doris Morris leaned toward me in a confidential way. "If you're smart, you'll stay away from the bum. He's a real opportunist. Take my word."

"I'll remember that," I said to her. "Good-bye, Miss Morris."

As Doris Morris disappeared down the street, I suddenly became depressed. So I decided to stroll over to Otter Pond—a place that Arnold and I used to go last winter. We would take bags of bread and cracked corn and feed all the birds who gathered there. Ducks, geese, swans. And while I had loved the little mallards, Arnold had preferred the swans. "They're almost like dogs," he'd said to me. "They eat right out of your hand. They follow you up the street."

I walked up Main Street until I reached the pond. And then I sat down on one of the benches they have there. Miss Morris' story had depressed me terribly, but I didn't know why. I mean, it was a success story, so I didn't know why it should give me feelings of despair. Boy, I thought, is she a tough lady. I bet no one takes advantage of *her*.

It was late June, all the little ducklings had been hatched, and dozens of them were swimming around with their mothers. I wished I had brought some bread for them. And, more than anything, I wished that Arnold was by my side. I thought of him standing by the pond last January, in the freezing weather, with two swans eating cracked corn from his hand. "They'll bite you," I had said. "Please be careful, Arnold. I know you love swans, but they can be vicious."

Arnold had turned and smiled at me. "That's a

contradiction, darling. If you love something, it is never vicious."

It was such an Arnold thing to say—such an Arnold kind of thought. For reasons that had never been clear to me, Arnold didn't understand that there was cruelty in the world. Or dishonesty. Or vice. He saw everything through smooth, invisible, rose-colored glasses— and yet was that really so bad? He would smile at people on the street, perfect strangers, and they would smile back. He was patient and gentle with moronic clerks in stores. He phoned his mother in Kansas every Sunday, year in, year out. Arnold Bromberg loved his mother, and me, and all the animals in the world— swans especially. Doris Morris would have considered him a perfect candidate for Scientific Religion. Positive thinking.

14

I WAS SITTING on Jerry Malone's water bed, watching him type furiously on an old electric machine he had set up on the card table. He was wearing jeans and a shirt, his feet were bare, and he was typing away like mad. You had to admire his industry, and you also had to admire the fact that he was doing the whole thing off the top of his head. My book, I mean. *Savage Sunset*.

Jerry had phoned that morning and asked me to bring him a cheeseburger, a malted, and two typewriter ribbons. He was really into the book now and didn't want to go out for food or supplies. He was averaging twenty pages a day, he said. His pace was good.

It was July, and summer had descended upon the Hamptons in its usual hot, humid, crowded way. What I mean is, summer is the time when most of us locals try to fade into the woodwork. The streets of Sag Harbor become jammed with tourists, there is no place to park, and all these people walk up and down the streets, looking at shop windows, and sometimes going inside, but never buying anything.

"I'll stop for lunch in a second," Jerry said, over the sound of the typewriter. "Just bear with me."

I watched him type—realizing that he typed the way I did, with the two middle fingers of each hand. A touch typist he was not. But he did go like wildfire.

I went over and stood by the window, where there was a breeze. It was a hot day, but I was wearing a pair of overalls and one of my father's shirts. Fat Clothes. I had gained twenty pounds. Don't you want to look stunning when you arrive in Zurich? Amanda Starcross would ask me all the time. No, Rita Formica would reply. I want to eat.

Two days ago I had done an amazing thing—which was to take the bus into New York, meet Corry at Rockefeller Center, and apply for a passport. It hadn't even occurred to me that I would need a passport to go abroad for one weekend, but Corry had straightened me out on this. So I had filled out the application form and had my photo taken—and then Corry and I walked over to Swissair, to inquire about the plane ticket. It did indeed cost eight hundred dollars to go to Zurich, round trip.

"I don't get paid for my book until I hand it in," I said to Corry. "So how am I going to purchase the ticket?"

She was stumped, but only for a second. "My mother's MasterCard. I'll forge her signature."

"Won't there be hell to pay?"

"Of course, but by the time the bill comes, you will have given me the money. I'll pay her back."

"With what excuse?"

"Who knows? I'll think of something."

We had wound up at a coffee shop in the west fifties, a crummy joint, but a place where they would let us sit and talk. I had not told Corry that Jerry Malone was writing my book, nor had I told her I intended to sleep with him. Corry was too much of a feminist to tolerate such news.

Corry had broken up with Ronald Studebaker, the paleontologist, and now she was at loose ends for the summer. She was spending most of her time at The Women's Alliance, which is a feminist headquarters in the East Village. "What do you do there?" I had asked her. "Lick envelopes," she had replied. "Answer the phone."

I have not yet described Corry here—but if you think of her as my opposite, you'll have it down pat. Skinny, pretty, aggressive, logical. Terrific clothes.

We sat over coffee for a long time, gossiping about the kids in Sag Harbor, the kids at her private school, and things in general. Then Corry said to me, "When exactly are you going to Zurich? Do you know the date?"

"Well no," I had replied. "I don't."

"You'll have to make the plane reservation well in advance."

"I know, Corry, I know."

"And you'll need some Swiss money. Some francs."

"Where do I get those?"

"I'll get them for you down on Wall Street, near my father's office. The thing is, you really should know when you're going."

I looked her straight in the eye. "August 29th."

"August 29th?"

"The 30th is Arnold's birthday. I'll be there for that."

"And how do you intend to *find* Arnold?"

"I'll find him," I muttered. "If I have to go to the police, I'll find him."

"The police may not be willing to help you."

"Then I'll hire a detective."

"In the space of one weekend?"

"Why are you putting such a damper on all this?' I almost shouted. "Why are you trying to discourage me?"

"Rita, Rita," said Corry, sounding like somebody's mother. "If you're really going to Zurich for a weekend, you have to do some more thinking about it."

"What would you suggest?"

"First, that you phone Arnold's parents in Kansas and see if they know where he is. I mean, wouldn't that be the first step?"

I had to admit she was right. Which was the thing about Corry—she always thought things through. I, on the other hand, thought nothing through. My heart ruled my head, so to speak. I was not practical.

That evening, while my parents were watching television, I pulled the phone into my room on its long cord, shut the door, and asked for Directory Assistance in Topeka, Kansas. There was only one Bromberg in the directory, and the operator gave me the number at once. Trembling a little, I dialed it.

The person who answered the phone was a sweet, gentle, rather vague lady. Mrs. Bromberg. At the sound of her voice, a shiver went through me. I was talking to my prospective mother-in-law.

"Mrs. Bromberg," I said, "you don't know me,

but I'm a friend of Arnold's. I live on Long Island, New York, and, uh, I very much need to know where Arnold is. Has he been in touch with you?"

"Who did you say you were, dear?" said the vague lady. "Where did you say you lived?"

"Sag Harbor. On Long Island. New York."

"What harbor, dear? This connection isn't very good."

"Sag," I said. "Sag. As in, his spirits *sagged*."

"Your spirits are sagging, dear?" said Mrs. Bromberg. "I'm so sorry to hear that."

We must have talked that way for five minutes, me trying to explain where Sag Harbor was, and Mrs. Bromberg asking me what was sagging. Finally, Arnold's father, the minister, got on the phone—and he was a hundred percent more rational. But alas, the Reverend Bromberg had no idea where his son was, except that his son was traveling in Europe. "We've had some postcards from Switzerland," said Reverend Bromberg. "Very nice postcards, too."

I was really depressed when I hung up the phone. Because the whole thing was beginning to seem impossible.

"OK," said Jerry Malone, bringing me back to the present. "I'm ready for lunch."

Feeling strangely domestic, I went to the kitchen and put Jerry's cheeseburger on a paper plate. Then I poured his malted into a beer mug. As far as housekeeping went, he certainly was not well equipped. "You need a few more dishes," I said as I brought him his lunch. "Your kitchen is rather bare."

He took the food from me, and made room for it on the card table. "I guess you have more things in your city apartment," I offered. "More dishes."

He took a bite of the cheeseburger. "There is no city apartment. This one is *it*, sweetheart. This is where I live."

I sat down on the water bed and stared at him. "How come?"

"Because I'm poor, that's how come. I can't afford to live in the city."

"But you do go in once a week?" I said hopefully. "To see your agent and everything?"

"My agent skipped town a year ago, taking with him the funds of the agency. So now he's my ex-agent."

I didn't know what to say after that, so I just sat there as Jerry finished his cheeseburger. He looked angry and bored. And tired. He had been working on my book round the clock.

This was the first time I had been with Jerry since the night when I had been sick in his bathroom. And I was steeling myself to make out with him on the water bed. A bargain is a bargain, I said to myself. The man is working like a dog on your book. You owe him something.

Trying to be seductive, I reclined backward on the bed. Underneath me, there was a sloshing sound. I wondered if I was too heavy for this particular bed, and if it would collapse under the weight of the two of us. I had a terrible image of Jerry and me being engulfed in water at some critical moment. "Wouldn't you be more comfortable over here?" I said to him. "On the bed?"

He came over to the bed and stretched out next to me. We lay there for a while, side by side, not touching. What's wrong? said my inner voice. Why isn't he making a pass at me? Darling, said Amanda Starcross, *try* to be more seductive.

I leaned over Jerry and looked into his eyes. They were dark purple, the color of grapes, and the expression in them was not friendly. "Would you like to kiss me?" I said. "It might help you relax."

"Do you find me attractive?" Jerry asked.

Unprepared for the question, I said, "No."

He winced. "Well, at least you're honest."

Trying to recover myself, I said, "Jerry, please don't get me wrong. Because you are attractive, very very attractive. It's just that *I* don't find you attractive. But to anyone else, you would be."

I lay back down on the bed, flat on my back. "I am available to you if you want to make out, Jerry. Here I am."

"Thanks a bunch."

"I beg your pardon?"

He turned over on his side, propped himself up on one elbow, and said, "Your offer has all the excitement of an afternoon of necrophilia."

"*What?*"

"God, Rita, where did you grow up? In a convent? And how old are you anyway? What's your real age?"

"I was just seventeen," I confessed. "A few months ago."

For a moment, memories of my very depressing seventeenth-birthday party swam before my eyes. Me and Mom and Dad in a Chinese restaurant in Southampton. And no message from Arnold.

"Seventeen?" he said. "You look older."

"I know, but I'm not."

"Well, maybe that explains it." He stood up and ran a hand through his hair. "Look, do you want to read what I've done so far? I'm very deeply into the book."

"Sure, I'd like to. Are you really averaging twenty pages a day?"

"Yep, that's my quota. If you don't work fast, the work doesn't pay."

As images of seduction on a water bed faded away from me, I rose to my feet and joined Jerry at the card table. "Here are the first fifty pages," he said. "I think they're pretty good."

I read the first chapter of *Savage Sunset* with a certain

amount of admiration. Because Jerry really knew this form very well. By page five, Temple Shannon was being raped on the third floor of the White House by Chance Darby. "Her breasts were naked now," I read, "and his manhood swelled as he gazed at them. By God, he would have this wench or die! She was a locked door, just waiting to be rammed."

I shuddered and kept on reading. The rape/seduction was much more explicit than I would have made it, but what the hell. Jerry obviously knew what he was doing. Then I came to the scene where Temple knocks out Chance Darby with a brass candlestick and steals into President Lincoln's quarters. In my last version, I had had the two of them, Temple and the President, having a glass of sherry together and talking. But Jerry had Temple disrobing in front of President Lincoln— taking her clothes off.

"Oh, no," I said. "This isn't right."

"What isn't right?" Jerry asked.

"You've got her taking off her clothes in front of the President of the United States."

"Exactly. Read on."

I read a few more paragraphs and felt myself going pale. "Jerry! You've got her seducing the President!"

Jerry Malone winked at me. "*That'll* keep them interested. *N'est-ce pas?*"

I rose to my feet and began to pace the room. "But that's not historically accurate! And also, why would she do such a thing?"

"She's just been seduced by Chance," said Jerry. "She's still horny. And if she sleeps with the President, he will give her an escort through enemy lines. To find her brother."

I was growing more and more upset. "It isn't historically accurate. Miss Morris won't like it at all."

"She'll like it, baby. It's very original."

"But it isn't true! President Lincoln would *never* allow himself to be seduced by a female spy who's just been raped on the third floor of the White House. It isn't in character. He was very pure."

"How do you know that?"

"I don't know how I know it, I just do! He was a very pure man. He didn't sleep with female spies."

Jerry put his arm around my shoulder and walked me to the door. "Don't worry about it, sweetheart. Just leave everything to me."

"But this is my book you're writing!"

"No," he said, "it isn't. Not anymore."

There was, unfortunately, some truth to that statement. So we walked out to the hallway, and it was obvious that he wanted me to leave. But before I left, there was something I had to know.

"Jerry," I said, "I want to ask you something important. Something that matters a lot to me."

He gazed at me. "OK, shoot."

"Why were you so eager to make out with me in the beginning? Why did you go to so much trouble?"

"Trouble?" he said. In the dim light of the hallway,

his eyes looked more purple than ever. Dark and mysterious.

"Well, yes. The expensive restaurants, the little notes, the bunch of flowers. Why were you so eager to have an affair?"

He shrugged. "I'm a horny person, Rita, and fat girls turn me on. The trouble is, there aren't too many around these days. Every girl you meet is a size six or something."

I felt like he had hit me in the face with a wet glove. A very old wet glove. "Thank you for your honesty," I said. "It's very refreshing."

He grinned. "We aim to please, sweetheart. We aim to please."

15

THAT NIGHT I sat with my mother in the living room, watching an old film on television—*Wuthering Heights*, with Merle Oberon and Laurence Olivier. My mother has seen this film a dozen times, and I have seen it twice. Nevertheless, we were both watching. It was my father's poker night, and Mom and I were alone.

We had had roast chicken with vegetables for dinner, but I had only taken a few bites. And when my mother brought out a bowl of diet tapioca pudding, decorated with cherries, I had only stared at it. Because, for the first time in months, my appetite was gone. I had looked at the bowl of tapioca as though it were a bowl of soft white plaster. "I'm a horny person," I heard Jerry Malone saying, "and fat girls turn me on."

OK, I said to myself, so now you're both even. You told *him* what you thought, and he told *you*. You don't find *him* attractive, and the only reason he wanted *you* is that you're fat. Fat girls turn him on. Baby whales.

On the TV screen Laurence Olivier and Merle Oberon were standing on a hill, looking out into the distance. Merle Oberon was leaning against Laurence Olivier and her hair was blowing in the wind. They were terribly in love. In England, on a moor.

I looked at my mother and saw that there were tears in her eyes. "Oh, Mom," I said, "please. It hasn't gotten sad yet."

"I know. It's just that they're so beautiful together."

The music swelled and Laurence Olivier kissed Merle Oberon. They were, indeed, very much in love. And it's true that they were beautiful. But every time my mother watched this movie, she cried. She would cry, very softly, from the beginning right through to the end.

Laurence Olivier was leaving Merle Oberon. She

had gotten herself involved with David Niven, and Olivier, the outcast Gypsy boy, couldn't fit in. But he would show her. Yes! He would go away, make his fortune, and return rich and powerful.

All of a sudden I realized something. And it was so important that I left the living room and went into the kitchen, to be alone. Because I understood why my mother watched this movie, and why she would go on watching it for the rest of her life. She watched *Wuthering Heights* for the same reason the housewives of America read historical romance: Because it gave her something she didn't have.

What *was* this something? Not just sex. And not romantic seduction, either, because Miss Morris was right—the flutes-and-violins kind of seduction didn't exist. What was it that everyone wanted, then?

"I'm a horny person," Jerry said in my mind, "and fat girls turn me on. The trouble is, there aren't too many around these days." It was like he had been discussing vintage cars or something. Fords with rumble seats.

I drank a glass of water, and then a second glass. The word I wanted was on the tip of my tongue, but I couldn't get it. From *Wuthering Heights* all the way to *Savage Sunset*, there was something in romantic fiction that women didn't get from real life.

I drank a third glass of water and went back to the living room. Heathcliff had returned to the house on the moors, rich and successful. Everything had changed. He was master now—handsome, and rather cruel.

My mother was on her second handkerchief. She wasn't hysterical or anything, she was just crying softly and privately.

The movie went on and on, and my mind kept wandering away from it. How could Arnold forget my birthday? His was written on my heart in blood. I thought of Arnold and Rose shopping together on the Bahnhofstrasse. I saw them riding across Zurich in a little blue tram. Perhaps by now they had taken an apartment together. Perhaps by now they were . . . married.

I sat straight up on the couch and put that thought out of my mind. Think positively, I said to myself, think of Doris Morris. Doris Morris went from rags to riches just by the quality of her thinking. You can do the same. By thinking positively, you will get to Zurich in time for Arnold's birthday on August 30th.

I must have dozed off sitting next to my mother, because when I woke, Merle Oberon was dying in a big four-poster bed, and Laurence Olivier was standing by her side stricken with grief. "I cannot live without my life!" Laurence Olivier cried in anguish. "I cannot die without my soul!"

It was then that my father walked through the front door. He had had a few beers with his poker friends and was very cheerful. He was wearing a red baseball cap, backward. "Hi there, pussycat!" he said to my mother. And to me, he said, "What's up, doc?"

16

ARNOLD'S POSTCARDS had stopped coming. I went to the post office every day—sometimes twice a day—but they had ceased. And to tell you that this made me nervous is like describing the tip of an iceberg. I was in a panic.

It was August 10th, my ticket to Zurich had been purchased by Corry, my passport had arrived in the mail, and my bag was packed—a small overnight case containing only the essentials: A sweater and a raincoat, a new nightgown, and five maps of Zurich. But the postcards were no longer coming, and I didn't know what to do. "Should I cancel?" I asked Corry over the phone. "Should I call the whole thing off?"

"You've gone this far," she said. "Keep on going."

My plan was to tell my parents that I was spending a three-day weekend with Corry, depart for the city on a bus—the afternoon of August 29th—but get off at Kennedy airport instead. Corry would meet me there and help me get on the plane, and if my mother called over the weekend, she would say I was napping.

Or shopping. Or soaking in the tub. Her parents would be in Nantucket that weekend, so she would be the only one home. It seemed like a foolproof plan.

Every night I would open the small suitcase I had packed and inspect its contents. The pretty nightgown, the raincoat, the five maps of Zurich. Somehow this ritual made me feel better—as though the suitcase were a friend who would not desert me.

How did I intend to find Arnold over the space of a three-day weekend? By checking out every inexpensive hotel in Zurich—assisted, I hoped, by a taxi driver. And if that failed, by going to the American Embassy. I myself would stay at any hotel that had a vacancy. . . . I must confess to you that these were all Corry's ideas, not mine. Her thoughts had been going full steam ahead.

Then there was Jerry Malone, who was writing *Savage Sunset* as though his electric typewriter were a weapon. I had told him I was leaving for Europe on August 29th, and he had promised faithfully to have the book finished on August 26th. That would leave only three days in which to hand in the manuscript, get paid, pay Jerry, and give eight hundred dollars to Corry at the airport. What would happen to Corry when her mother received the MasterCard bill for the plane ticket, I did not want to contemplate.

Since our last argument over *Savage Sunset*, Jerry had refused to let me see the manuscript. It was coming along fine, he said, going like wildfire. But he did not want my criticisms to get in his way. The only thing that disturbed me was that Jerry often smoked a joint before he worked, to relax himself, to get into the mood. It did not seem like a good method for writing a book.

My relationship with Jerry had changed so drastically that we were now like an old married couple. We argued a lot. I brought him cheeseburgers and took his laundry to the Laundromat. Once a week, I tidied up his apartment—hanging up clothes, doing the dishes, trying to make order. And, typically, he was not grateful for these services at all. We had long conversations on the water bed—about the nature of historical romance—Jerry smoking a joint, me smoking a Kool, and neither of us agreeing with the other. He thought the books were something for women to devour, like candy bars, while I kept feeling that there was a real message at the heart of them. What it was, however, I did not know.

On August 26th, I went to Jerry's apartment at three in the afternoon, and proudly he handed me the manuscript. It was four hundred pages long, neatly typed, and packed into a cardboard box. There it was, *Savage Sunset*, our creation. "I'm so excited," I said. "It's like the birth of a child or something."

"Right," he said, "like a new baby. A homely baby, but a baby nevertheless. Take it home, read it, and then give me a call. If you find any discrepancies, make a note of them. Do some copyediting for me."

I put the box under my arm and walked toward the door. "What kind of discrepancies?"

"You know. Anything that doesn't jibe. If I have Temple wearing a red dress in one scene, and then a pink dress a few minutes later, that's a discrepancy. Make a note of things like that and I'll fix them."

I gazed at Jerry Malone, who was wearing only his pajama bottoms, and who looked exhausted, and said, "I'll always be grateful to you Jerry, for the rest of my life. I mean it. You've done a fantastic job."

"We aim to please, sweetheart," he said wearily. "We aim to please."

That night, while my parents entertained friends in the living room, I locked myself in my room and began to read *Savage Sunset*. The opening was good— swift, tight, suspenseful. And the rape of Temple Shannon by Chance Darby was sort of breathtaking, though crude. Then, alas, Jerry had Temple seducing President Lincoln, in order to get an escort through enemy lines. At least, I thought, *at least* he does not describe the sex in this scene. He just has her taking off her clothes in a seductive manner and the President going pale. At least the chapter ends with her taking the President's hand and leading him to a big fluffy bed.

I read on. Through battle scenes and love scenes.

Through scenes where the lusty Tawny O'Rourke impersonates Temple to save her from being raped by the entire Rebel army. Then I came to a dead halt. Temple Shannon had gotten pregnant by Abraham Lincoln. Her decision now was whether or not to bear the child. "No!" I said aloud. "Absolutely not!" I raced into the hallway, dragged the phone into my room, and shut the door.

Jerry was asleep when I rang him and sounded irritable. "Who is this?" he said. "What time is it?"

"It's me," I said furiously, "and I'm reading my book. And I will not allow Temple Shannon to get pregnant by Abraham Lincoln. It's sick! It's crude! And it isn't even historically accurate. How could you have done this, Jerry? It's wrecked the book."

"Calm down," he said, "calm down. Let me get my eyes open."

"You stinker! You've wrecked the goddam book. President Lincoln would never, never do these things. The whole idea of it makes me ill. What kind of a crude mind do you have, anyway? How many joints did you smoke while writing this stuff?"

"If you will just . . ."

"No," I said, "I won't. I won't calm down. Because you've wrecked my book."

"Honey," said Jerry, "it isn't your book. It's nobody's book—just a piece of trash from which we are going to make a few bucks. What does it matter *what*

President Lincoln does to Temple Shannon? Who cares?"

"*I* care," I said, "because this is my first published book and you've ruined it."

"But your name won't even be on it!"

"Maybe not, but I'll know it's my book all the same. And every time I see it in the dime store, or the supermarket, I'll feel ashamed."

"Oh, honey . . ."

"It's true. I'll feel ashamed. And I'm not going to hand it in to Miss Morris."

There was a meaningful pause on the other end of the phone. "Then how do you get to Europe on August 29th? Tell me that."

"I don't know," I said bleakly. "I don't know anything anymore."

"You're going to have to reconsider all this," Jerry said. "Because, baby doll, you owe me a thousand dollars. And I really do insist that you pay me."

"Take it out in trade," I said. And, as there was a gasp on the other end of the phone, I hung up. I didn't even know what "take it out in trade" meant, but it was an expression Jerry used all the time.

I went over and sat down on my bed, feeling like someone had kicked me in the stomach. I simply could not hand this book in to Doris Morris, because despite the fact that Jerry had written it, and the Starcross name would be on it, the book was still mine. My responsibility, my task, my assignment. And I had wanted it to be good—hack work, but good all the same. Arnold, I said silently, I'm in real trouble. Tell me what to do.

For the very first time since he had left Sag Harbor, I heard Arnold's voice inside my head. It was like we were on the phone together or something. The connection wasn't great, but he was on the other end of some very profound psychic telephone. "Go to Miss Morris," Arnold's voice said to me, "and tell her the truth. Truth always wins in the end."

17

MISS MORRIS WAS ensconced in one of her Victorian couches and I was sitting on a straight-backed chair. The maid had just served us glasses of iced tea, and despite the humid day the room seemed airy and cool. Flamboyant as always, Miss Morris was wearing one of her bright blouses with short black shorts. High-heeled, open-toed shoes. Four gold bracelets on one arm. "So how's it coming?" she said. "You should be finished pretty soon."

"I am finished," I said in a small voice. "I mean, the book is finished. But I've got a problem."

Doris Morris chuckled and took a sip of her tea. "What's the matter?" she said jovially. "Couldn't you make it raunchy enough?"

I made myself look Miss Morris straight in the eye. "I have something to tell you."

"So?" she replied. "Fire away."

"The . . . the book is finished, but I didn't write it. Jerry wrote it. And he was stoned a good part of the time."

Miss Morris put her glass of iced tea on the table. Very carefully, she patted her lips with a napkin. "And you were going to pass the book off as yours?"

"Yes. That's what I intended to do. But he's made a mess of it, and I don't want it published. He's made it dirty, and historically wrong, and I just can't stand it. If you want to sue me or something, you can. The whole thing is my fault."

Doris Morris was regarding me carefully, scrutinizing me, sizing me up. "Tell me what you needed the money for. I'd like to know."

It was then that I burst into tears—crying like some kind of a five-year-old, crying so hard that Miss Morris had to ring for the maid, who brought me a box of Kleenex. "Ah, come on now," she said to me. "It can't be that bad. Nothing ever is."

But once I had started, I couldn't stop. Because I was crying for myself, and Arnold, and our love affair, and for the fact that I would never get to Switzerland. I was crying because I was seventeen and Arnold was thirty-three, and because our love had been doomed from the beginning. My parents had been right. Arnold was too old for me, and I was too young for him, and the entire Atlantic Ocean separated us. And so I cried.

"Come on now, kid," said Miss Morris sternly, "that's enough. Tell me what's going on."

After blowing my nose and wiping my eyes, I began to tell Doris Morris the history of me and Arnold Bromberg. I told her how we had met, how we had fallen in love, and how my parents had managed to separate us. I told her of Arnold's departure for Europe and how, at this very moment, he was probably living in some seedy hotel in Zurich. I told her of my plans to join him for a weekend—just one weekend—so that we could be together. On his birthday.

To my amazement, I saw that Miss Morris' eyes were damp. "God," she said, "what a touching story. You haven't made it up?"

I shook my head.

"And you say this guy left you because he didn't want to ruin your life?"

I nodded, too upset to speak.

"God," said Doris Morris, "that's really touching. Does he love you as much as you love him?"

I began to cry again, but this time very softly.

116

"Amazing," said Miss Morris. "Like Romeo and Juliet or something. Like Orpheus and Eurydice."

"Who?"

"Never mind. It doesn't matter. The problem is, how are you going to get to Switzerland?" She smiled. "For the weekend."

"I don't know! That's what's so terrible, Miss Morris. I don't know. I guess . . . I guess I just can't get there."

She gave me a cool look. "You'll get there, all right."

"Pardon me?"

"You're going," she said firmly. "You're going to Zurich if I have to charter the Concorde. Wait here for a moment. I'll be right back."

As I sat in the living room with my mouth open, Miss Morris disappeared upstairs. In a minute she was back again, a manila folder and a large checkbook under her arm.

She sat down opposite me and opened the checkbook. "Now, first things first. How much did you agree to pay that joker?"

"Jerry?"

"Yeah, Jerry. The Don Juan who lives over the health food store."

"A thousand dollars."

"Fine. And how much is the plane fare?"

I wasn't sure I was hearing Miss Morris correctly, but I said, "Eight hundred."

"OK, fine. One thousand plus eight hundred, plus a little extra for contingencies, brings us up to around twenty-five hundred." She opened the large checkbook and began to write out a check.

"Oh no!" I said. "No, Miss Morris. I can't let you do that."

"Oh, yes you can," she replied. "We'll call it a business loan and you can pay me back someday. When you're a published author."

She signed the check and handed it to me. Then she opened the manila folder. "This is the contract you signed with me. Or rather, it *was* the contract you signed with me, because now we are tearing it up."

Doris Morris tore up my contract, handed me the pieces, and said, "So go to Europe for the weekend and have a good time. You remind me of myself— would you believe that? Only many years ago. A long long time ago."

As Miss Morris and I shook hands, a lump came into my throat as big as a golf ball. "How can I ever repay you?" I asked.

"By being happy," she replied. And then—with all of her bracelets jangling—she quickly left the room.

18

ON AUGUST 29TH, at four in the afternoon, I sat on a crowded bus heading for New York City. I felt like a dreamer having a very vivid dream, the only problem being that I could not wake up and start over. My small suitcase was on the rack above my head, I had a magazine and two packs of chewing gum—to keep me from smoking—but I felt very very unreal.

In order not to arouse suspicion when I left home, I had departed in blue jeans and a shirt, my hair pulled back with a ribbon. "Good-bye, dear," my mother had said. "Have a good time. And give my love to Corry." She was cooking something on the stove.

I stood in the doorway and looked at her, my eyes brimming with tears. "Good-bye, Mom. Take care of yourself."

"What's that, dear?" she said absently, as she stirred whatever it was she was cooking.

"I said take care of yourself. And tell Daddy the same. To take care."

My mother sprinkled some salt into the cooking pot. "I never know how much salt to put in this stew."

I went over and kissed her on the back of the neck. "Good-bye, Mom," I said in a strangled voice.

"You'd think the recipe would say how much *salt*," she said. "Good-bye, sweetie. Have fun."

As the bus barreled along the expressway, I opened my purse and took out Arnold's postcards, held together with a rubber band. On the eve of my departure, Corry had phoned and asked me to bring them to the airport. "I think I know how to find Arnold!" she had whispered into the phone. "The key is in the postcards." Wearily, I had told Corry that the majority of the postcards only showed swans, but she insisted. "Bring the postcards to the airport," she said. "I mean it, Rita. This is vital."

One by one, I went through the postcards as the bus rattled and swayed. Churches, museums, the Bahnhofstrasse, the railway station, and many many postcards of swans. I couldn't imagine what Corry had in mind.

As the bus pulled into the vast complex of Kennedy airport, I began to feel ill. Rita Formica, I said to myself, what are you doing? How did you get into this? Did it ever occur to you that Arnold might not even *be* in Zurich anymore? Did it ever occur to you that you might get stuck over there? You should have made out a will before you left, you should have torn up the love letters Arnold wrote you last January. Suppose your mother finds those letters? Suppose the plane crashes? Well, if it crashes your troubles will be over, and people will remember you with sadness and respect. You will be the Amelia Earhart of Sag Harbor.

Corry was waiting for me at the Swissair counter, and I must say that she looked nervous. "You're supposed to check in at six, and it's a quarter to six right now," she said to me. "Your plane leaves at eight. It's a 747, one of the big ones. Did you bring the postcards? Did you remember your passport?"

I hugged her and said, "Be calm, be calm. Everything's going to be all right. Yes, I brought the postcards. I brought everything."

"You have to check in," she repeated. "Then we can go have coffee or something."

I checked in with Swissair, said that I would keep my overnight bag with me, and was handed a boarding pass for the plane. "Kindly be at gate 32 at seven o'clock," the clerk said to me. "And have a good flight."

Corry and I made our way to the nearest coffee shop, and the fact that she was so nervous made me feel calmer. Yes, I told her again, I had brought my passport, and the Swiss francs, and my maps of Zurich. I had brought everything.

"First things first," I said to Corry, after we had ordered our coffee. I opened my purse, took out eight one-hundred-dollar bills, and handed them to her. "For the plane ticket. Did the MasterCard bill come?"

"Not yet, not yet. Where are the postcards?"

I gave them to her. "Here. But I still don't know what you're aiming at."

Corry spread out the postcards on the table, putting them into different piles. The pile with the swans was the biggest. She took a swan postcard, turned it over, and pulled out a magnifying glass from her purse. "Aha!" she said.

"What is it?" I asked. "What do you see?"

"Do you see what the printing says on all of these swan cards?"

I looked carefully at the message side of each card. "It says, 'Swans,' Corry. And then it just says, 'Zurich.' "

"But what does it say *under* the word Zurich?"

I borrowed the magnifying glass from her and looked closely. "It says . . . Utoquai. What does that mean?"

"I don't know," Corry said excitedly. "It's a place or something. But why would so many cards show just one place?"

"I don't know."

"Because he goes there a lot, that's why!" she said triumphantly. "Find the Utoquai, and you will find Arnold."

"But that's fantastic!"

"It's not. It's logical."

"But what is an *Utoquai*?"

"An embankment, obviously. A place where people sit and watch swans. You always told me that Arnold loves swans."

"God, Corry. It's such a long shot."

She gave me a hard look. "Do you have any others?"

At seven o'clock, the two of us stood at gate 32. "This is where I leave you," Corry said. "Now, be careful, use your head, and don't talk to strange men. I asked my father last night, quite casually, what the Swiss are like, and he said that they're weird. He's been to Zurich on business. Don't let anyone pick you up or anything. And for God's sake, don't miss the plane back!"

I embraced her. "I love you," I said.

"Me too," she said gruffly. "Just don't let any of those Swiss men pick you up."

I watched Corry disappear down the corridor. Then, along with hundreds of other people, I went into the lounge at gate 32. I felt like I had eaten a bad oyster or something. Queasy and faint. Arnold, I thought, help me get through this experience. Because I am doing it for us.

19

MY SEAT WAS in a nonsmoking section, in the front of the plane, on the aisle. And my neighbor was a person named Floyd Hemingway who said that he was in beauty products. I had been on jet planes before, to visit my grandmother in Florida, but this was not like that experience at all.

To begin with, I did not feel I was in a plane, but in a hotel that was about to levitate into the sky. A big hotel where four hundred people were placing orders for drinks, and being handed magazines, and chatting amiably with each other. I turned around to look behind me, and could barely see the end of the plane—that's how long the goddam thing was. And, while I am usually not afraid of flying, suddenly I was. My neighbor, Mr. Hemingway, obviously wanted to be pals. "Is this your first flight?" he asked.

"Certainly not," I said coldly. "I go abroad every year."

Mr. Hemingway went back to reading his magazine. Then stewardesses began shutting all the doors, and the engines revved up, and I felt more queasy than ever. "May I buy you a drink?" Mr. Hemingway asked, obviously thinking that I was older than seventeen. "Well . . ." I said. "OK. Make it a double scotch."

I was already on my guard against Floyd Hemingway, who, for all I knew, could be some kind of pervert or kidnapper. But I changed my mind when our drinks arrived, because he was so courteous. "Cheers," he said, raising his glass to me. "You too," I said. "Good luck."

I am not going to bore you here with descriptions of transatlantic travel. Suffice it to say that once our hotel had taken off—straight up into the blue—the whole experience became very busy. There were drinks to be drunk, and magazines to be read, and Swissair literature to be perused, and games for children, and packs of cards for adults, and dinner to be ordered. Etc. "They certainly keep a person *busy* on one of these flights," I said to Mr. Hemingway. "I guess it's so we don't have time to think about death."

Floyd Hemingway gave me a strange look and went back to drinking his drink. He had wanted to be friendly at first, but now I suspect he was finding me a little odd. Also, since I never drink, the scotch was hitting me like a ton of bricks. I drank my drink and read my Swissair literature. I ate my superb, but tiny, Swissair dinner. After dinner, there was a movie.

Mr. Hemingway had put on some earphones, to listen to music, and his eyes were closed—so I had an opportunity to study him. A large heavy man with red cheeks. Around the age of my father. "What kind of beauty products are you in?" I asked him.

"What?" he said, taking off the earphones.

"I said, what kind of beauty products are you in?"

Mr. Hemingway brightened up at once. "Hair-brushes," he said. "The Dainty Doll hairbrush. It's selling like hotcakes."

"It's for a doll?"

"No, no. It's just a very small hairbrush, for the purse. We're introducing it to the European market this year."

"Sounds nice," I said politely.

"It is, it is."

"Are you any relationship to Ernest Hemingway?" I asked.

He looked surprised. "No. I'm not."

"Sorry. It's just that you look a little bit like him."

"Isn't he dead?" asked Mr. Hemingway, who obviously was not a reader of fiction.

"Oh, long dead," I replied. "Dead and buried. It's just that you resemble him."

I never made it through the movie, which was some kind of comedy with Goldie Hawn—because the scotch, plus the good meal, plus the steady sound of the engines, lulled me to sleep. A stewardess came and put a blanket over me and a small pillow under my head. And then I was gone.

I woke at daybreak to see a field of white clouds outside the window and a line of pink on the horizon. Mr. Hemingway was still asleep, snoring softly. Over the loudspeaker came the pilot's voice, telling us that we were flying over Ireland. A lump came into my throat as I realized the enormity of what I had just done. I, Rita Formica, from a small town on the end of Long Island, had just crossed the Atlantic.

I went off to the bathroom to freshen up, and the minute I was back in my seat I took out one of my maps of Zurich. Sure enough, there was the Uto-quai—and just as Corry had thought, it was an embankment on the shores of Lake Zurich. Whether or not Lake Zurich was close to the heart of the city, I could not figure out. I had a sudden image of myself sitting for twenty-four hours by the side of a lake.

Once again, Swissair kept us busy. Hot cloths were distributed to wipe our faces with, and chilled orange juice was served, and then a very nice breakfast. Fifty minutes later, we were landing at Kloten airport outside Zurich. It was the 30th of August, the morning of Arnold's birthday.

The plane taxied down the runway, and the minute it came to a halt people began to crowd the aisles, pulling on jackets and raincoats. I was in the midst of all this, pressed up against Mr. Hemingway. "I have a little present for you," he said. Upon which he handed me a Dainty Doll hairbrush.

"Thank you," I gasped, as the crush in the aisle got worse. "That's very thoughtful."

"Just a little souvenir," he said happily. "With the best wishes of Floyd Hemingway."

A short time later, I was standing in a huge airport—having gone through something called Passport Control, and then having gone down two escalators. It was ten in the morning, Zurich time, and four A.M. New York time, and I felt very odd. Jet lag, perhaps. Or just plain fear.

My problem was that I had no idea how to get into

Zurich, and that I was afraid to ask anyone. The only languages being spoken around me were French and German, and a few that I didn't recognize at all. Nobody looked friendly.

I saw the large, reassuring form of Mr. Hemingway heading across the airport, so I decided to follow him. He made straight for a platform that looked like an elegant version of a New York subway station, and then a shiny red train pulled up and he got on. Two cars down from him, I got on too. Using the rudimentary German I had studied last spring, at Peterson High, I read the signs on the train and knew that I was in the right place. The train went to Zurich.

Well, let me tell you. I had anticipated some kind of beautiful medieval scene outside the window—but as that train barreled into the city of Zurich, all I could think of was that Zurich looked like the Bronx. Factories, worn-out buildings, shabby streets. The sky was a gunmetal gray.

After ten minutes, the train pulled into a railway station, and as I debarked—with Mr. Hemingway just ahead of me—I stopped and caught my breath. Because I was standing in the biggest, most impressive railway station I had ever seen. It was like an entire city—a city covered by a glass roof, and filled with restaurants and shops, and newsstands and movie theaters, and flower stalls. High up, near the glass-domed ceiling, whole flocks of little birds were flying around.

Hot on the heels of Mr. Hemingway, I hurried through this enormous, echoing station and finally reached the street. Ahead of me, Mr. Hemingway was getting into a cab, and for just a moment I felt a stab of sorrow at seeing him depart. When the next cab rolled up, I jumped into it and threw my overnight bag down on the seat. *"Guten Morgen,"* I said carefully. "Me, American. Me, from New York."

"So hi there," said the cab driver. "My name is Max."

I was dumbfounded. "You speak English?"

He turned and grinned at me—a young man wearing a visored cap and a blue shirt. "So yes, I do. English I most definitely speak. Where do you go, miss? What is your pleasure?"

"The Utoquai," I said. "Near the lake."

"Sure thing, miss. But have you no hotel, no place where to drop your bag?"

"Not yet," I replied. "I'm only here for the weekend."

"From where, if I may ask?"

"Long Island," I said, as he started up the engine and pulled away from the curb. "It's near New York City."

"Ah, New York," said Max, in his strange accent.

"My uncle, once he went to New York. Very big, he said. Very dirty."

"True," I agreed, staring out of the taxi window. Was this Zurich? It looked just like any other city in the summer. Crowded, jammed with traffic, hot.

The cab made its way through the busy streets, veered to the left, crossed a little bridge—and then, suddenly, I saw a city that was built on the banks of a river, saw ancient buildings and spires, and heard church bells ringing. "What is *this*?" I asked.

"Zurich," said my friend Max. "The Old Town."

"But this is beautiful!"

"*Ja, ja,*" said my friend. "I shall agree."

I whipped out one of my maps. Yes, this was the River Limmat, and the street we were driving along was the Left Bank. There was the Fraumunster cathedral, and on my left the Grossmunster cathedral. There was the Water Chapel I had read about in books.

Max, whose full name was Max Schuler, guided the cab along the Left Bank, past several bridges, and onto a wide avenue. "Now," he said, "we approach the Zurichsee, or Lake Zurich if you will. It runs into the Limmat and, at this time of season, is ample with boats. Are you sure that is your destination?"

I decided to confide in Max Schuler. He was, after all, the only friend I had at the moment, and I needed him. "I'm trying to find someone in Zurich," I said, "and I've only got twenty-four hours in which to do it. It's an emergency."

Max paused for a stoplight. "Only twenty-four hours? Certainly, that is difficult. A young man, perhaps, you are looking for?"

"Yes. My fiancé."

He whistled through his teeth, a long, drawn-out whistle. "And you have come all the way from America for this venture?"

"Yes."

He turned around and handed me a card. "My card, with a phone number. If you need assistance within these twenty-four hours, I shall be glad to help you. My uncle would also be glad." He pulled over to a curb. "The Utoquai."

I looked at the Utoquai with a sinking heart. Because—just as Corry had thought—it was simply a stone embankment with some benches and a very long promenade. In the water were dozens of swans who looked brilliant against the gray sky. Most of the people sitting on the benches were old, and most of them had dogs.

I handed some Swiss money to Max Schuler. "Will you take the right amount? And of course, a tip too."

Carefully, Max selected one bill. "This will be sufficient. And may I wish you good fortune and good luck?"

He got out of the cab, came around and opened my door. "Your situation has impressed me," he said, "so that I hope you find your fiancé. Love is a scarcity in this world."

"Thank you," I said. "You've been terrific."

In a second, he was gone. And I was standing alone on the Utoquai.

I sat down on one of the benches, realizing how grubby I must look. What I really needed was a bath and a nap, but there wasn't time. I would sit here for most of the day, waiting for Arnold, and if he didn't show up I would call Max Schuler and have him take me to the American Embassy. Were embassies open on weekends? Oh God, oh God, I said to myself. Your plane goes back tomorrow morning. This is impossible, crazy, insane. Only a person in love would have done something like this. Only a fat girl.

I had saved some rolls from my Swissair breakfast, and there was a kiosk nearby that sold coffee. I went over and tried to ask for the coffee in German, but the woman selling it smiled and said, "Oh yes, miss, of course. Coffee sweet, with milk."

I returned to my bench on the Utoquai and sipped my coffee. I took the Dainty Doll hairbrush out of my purse and brushed my hair. The sky was so dark that I knew it was going to rain. And what then? Well, I had a raincoat with me, so I would put it on and continue to sit on my bench. I would give myself till six P.M.

The swans were gliding back and forth in the gloom. Across the lake were large, imposing stone buildings. The Old Town, where the churches were, was about a mile away. Gray skies and church bells, swans and cobbled streets. No wonder Arnold had come here.

I must have dozed off, because when I woke the sky had gone darker and a few drops of rain were falling. I looked at my watch. Four o'clock, Zurich time, and no Arnold. Where will you sleep tonight? my inner voice asked me. You can't sleep on a park bench. And suppose something terrible happens and you never get back home? Your parents will go into shock. Rita Formica, of all the crazy things you have ever done, this is the craziest.

And then I saw Arnold.

He was approaching from a distance, strolling along the promenade, so that the first thing I saw were his sneakers—white and dazzling in the gloom. He came closer and I saw that yes, indeed, it was him—wearing a wrinkled summer suit and carrying a brown paper bag. He was much taller than I had remembered, and much larger. His brown curly hair was bushier than before. He had no umbrella.

20

A WAVE OF EMOTION swept over me—excitement, relief, gratitude—but mostly joy at seeing Arnold

Bromberg again. How wonderful he looked! Tall, impressive, interesting. There was no one like him, and there never would be. He was *un original*.

Arnold walked over to an iron railing near the water and opened his paper bag. As though a signal had been given, around twenty swans sailed toward him. "Good girls," he said, "lovely girls. Here's your bread."

The swans seemed to know him well. Crowding around the embankment, they lifted their heads as Arnold dropped bread for them into the water. "Lovely creature," he said to one little swan, "here's your dinner."

It's crazy, but I was hesitant to approach him. I mean, we had been apart for seven months and I felt afraid. Also, his preoccupation with the swans was so great that I didn't know how to interrupt it. Whatever Arnold did, he did fully, even if it was just feeding swans.

All of the bread was gone. Turning the bag upside down, Arnold shook the last crumbs into the water. "No more," he said. "No more until tomorrow."

Trying to control my heart, which was beating like a drum, I rose to my feet and walked over to Arnold Bromberg. "Happy birthday," I said.

Like an actor in a slow-motion film, Arnold turned and stared at me. Then he clutched at his heart and staggered over to one of the benches. As though all the wind had been knocked out of him, he sank down.

"Arnold!" I said. "Are you all right? Don't be shocked, Arnold, please. It's just me, Rita. I've come for the weekend. Oh Arnold, are you OK? You look like you're going to faint."

I sat down next to him on the bench, afraid that he was going to have a stroke or something. Nervously, I patted his shoulder. "It's just me, Arnold, don't be shocked. Everything is all right."

He was weeping, his face in his hands, his shoulders moving up and down. Weeping with shock and amazement, and God knows what other emotions. I thought of my father, months ago, weeping in Mrs. Perlman's office.

"Arnold," I said, "please don't cry. Everything will be OK. I promise you."

But I was crying myself, crying for the whole seven months of our separation, and crying because I knew that I still loved him and would always love him. Nothing had changed for me.

We continued to cry together, and then his hand reached out for mine. "I wanted to look nicer for you," I said through my tears. "I'm sorry I don't look nicer."

"You look . . . beautiful," he said, wiping his tears.

"Do you feed the swans here every day?"

"Yes. I do."

"That's what Corry thought. That's how I found you."

It was raining now, and my hair was plastered to my forehead in long strings. Arnold's hair just seemed to get curlier in the rain, but mine hung down dismally. I lifted his hand to my lips and kissed it. "I still love you," I said. "I came to tell you that."

He began to cry again, so I put my arm around him and drew his head down on my shoulder. "It'll be all right," I said. "We'll work it out."

"I have a room nearby. In a *pension*, a boardinghouse."

"So let's go there. We'll catch pneumonia out here in the rain."

Arnold rose to his feet, crumpled up the paper bag, and deposited it in a trash basket. Holding hands, we began to walk toward his boarding house. Trying to simplify the story of how I found him, I told him about Corry's detective work and about a woman named Doris Morris lending me money for the plane. The story of the romances, and Jerry, was too complicated to go into.

As we paused for a stoplight, I said to Arnold. "Why did you stop sending me postcards?"

Arnold shook his head sadly. "Because I felt the whole thing was hopeless—that I should leave you in peace."

"Peace! I haven't had a moment's peace since you left. But not even a birthday card, Arnold?"

"I sent you a card. A birthday card with swans on it."

"Oh darling, I never got it."

Arnold looked like he was going to weep again, so I squeezed his hand and made us walk at a faster pace. We were both soaked from the rain.

The *pension*, or boardinghouse, was in a neighborhood called Bellerive, and it was simply a small building with a big, polished front door. Arnold led me into the hallway, and immediately a fat woman with blond hair in a bun confronted us. "My landlady," Arnold whispered.

"*Guten Abend*, Frau Schmidt," said Arnold.

"*Guten Abend,*" the woman replied. "And who, may I ask, is this?"

"A guest," Arnold said quickly. "A friend from America. We're just going upstairs for a cup of tea."

"*Ja, ja,*" said Frau Schmidt dubiously. "All well and good, Herr Bromberg. But you know the rules."

"A cup of tea," Arnold repeated firmly. "We were caught in the rain, and we require a cup of tea."

Frau Schmidt shrugged and went back to her parlor. "We're not allowed to have guests in our rooms," Arnold said as we climbed the staircase. "It's against the rules."

"God! What is this place, Arnold? A monastery?"

"It's just the Swiss," he said in a low voice. "They're puritanical."

Arnold's room, which was on the third floor, was so tiny that it could only hold a bed, a bureau, and one chair. The bathroom was down the hall. "I'll leave

137

the door open," said Arnold, "so Frau Schmidt won't be offended."

He had changed. I saw this at once as I sat down on his bed, and as he gave me a towel with which to dry my hair. He still looked large and bearish, tousled and innocent, but in some way that I couldn't define, he was different.

I dried my hair with his towel, and then I went down the hall to use the bathroom. Despite the fact that it was shared, it was very clean, with a deep, coffin-like tub.

I washed my hands and face, combed my hair, and put on a trace of lipstick. When I returned to Arnold's room, he was boiling water for tea on a small hot plate. "Does it cost much to live here?" I asked.

"No, no, it's very cheap. That's why I took it."

"And you're really not allowed to have guests?"

He smiled. "No. But I haven't wanted a guest till now."

A sudden thought entered my mind. "Where's Rose? If she's in Zurich, you'd better tell me."

"Rose?" said Arnold. "Rose who?"

"*Rose*. That woman you were in love with. The dancer."

Arnold looked baffled. "Why, I haven't seen her in years. I have no idea where she is."

"You told me once that she was in Europe."

"I did?"

"Yes, Arnold, you did."

"Rita dear, I haven't thought about Rose for a long time."

I studied him, to be sure he was telling the truth. He was. "Sorry," I said. "It's just my crazy imagination. It gets away from me."

Arnold handed me a cup of tea, and then he took his own cup and sat down on the chair. I sat on the edge of the bed, feeling uncomfortable. Out of place.

The room was terribly bare, with just two books and a photo of Arnold's mother on the bureau. His clothes hung neatly in a tiny curtained alcove. On the windowsill were some dishes and cups, a few forks, a packet of paper napkins. I walked over to the window and looked out. By stretching my neck a little, I could see the lake. "You've got a view," I said.

"Yes. I watch the sun come up every morning, over the Zurichsee. It's beautiful."

I turned and looked at him. "Oh Arnold, what are you doing here? I'm so baffled by everything."

"I had to get away from you," he said quietly, "so I came to Europe. I was given a small advance, you see, on my book."

"From a publisher?"

"Yes, a New York publisher. That's what I'm living on."

"But Arnold, how wonderful! The book on Bach, you mean?"

He nodded. "They want it done in a year, and I think I can do that."

I looked around the room. "But where do you work? This place is so small."

"I work at a library, a few blocks away. They've been awfully nice about it. They've given me a cubbyhole and a typewriter."

We could have been any two people talking over a cup of tea. Not Arnold and Rita, who had been such passionate lovers, but two acquaintances discussing a book on Bach. "Why Zurich?" I asked. "Why not Paris or Rome?"

Arnold finished his tea and put the cup down on the bureau. "I was restless after I left America, and I missed you so . . . painfully that I just kept traveling from place to place. Then I spent a week here, in Zurich, and happened to wander into the Fraumunster. Do you know what that is?"

"Yes. The cathedral on the right bank."

"Well, I happened to wander in there one morning, and the organist was practicing. I had never heard such skill before, never in my life. And the organ, Rita! It was built in the eighteenth century, and you simply cannot believe the sound!"

"You mean that you've stayed here to listen to an organ?"

"Right, right. The organist's name is Herr Kubli and he practices every morning at nine. I listen for an hour, and then I go to the library to work."

"So you've stayed here to listen to an organ," I said slowly. "At the Fraumunster. Well."

"I'll take you there tomorrow. You'll see what I mean."

"I'm leaving tomorrow," I said bleakly. "The plane goes at eleven in the morning."

All of a sudden Arnold and I realized that Frau Schmidt was standing outside the door. She had her arms folded across her bosom and looked like a sentinel or something. "Well," I said loudly, "I guess it's time for me to go. Will you escort me downstairs?"

Arnold smiled. "We'll go out to dinner. There's a nice restaurant around the corner."

As we passed Frau Schmidt in the hall, Arnold bowed. Frowning, Frau Schmidt watched us go down the stairs.

I had my raincoat on, and Arnold was wearing his too. It was dark, and the rain was soft and steady—blurring the lights of the traffic. Church bells were ringing. "Do the bells ring all the time?" I asked.

"No," Arnold said, "just at certain hours. Look darling, let's walk over to the Hotel Europa and see if we can get you a room. You can't stay with me, you know."

"Oh, of course not. God forbid I should sleep in your room."

"It's just the Swiss. They're like that."

"Yeah, but what are they like *underneath*?"

"That's a subject for another time."

Two blocks away was the tiny Hotel Europa, and Arnold had no trouble getting me a room. Speaking German, he dealt with the clerk and gave him some money. He seemed completely at ease doing all this, as though he had lived in Zurich for years.

As we sat over dinner in a small *stubli*, Arnold watched me. There was a candle on the table and it cast a flickering light. "You look so lovely," he said. "So young."

"I've gained twenty pounds."

He took my hand. "It doesn't matter. You're beautiful."

I had eaten almost nothing that day, and yet I wasn't hungry. I looked at my platter of veal and roast potatoes and felt nothing. Arnold was having a sandwich and a beer.

"You've changed," I said to him.

"How?" he asked.

"I don't know. Something is different."

Arnold was still holding my hand. And I realized that we had been together for hours now without kissing. "Are men allowed in ladies' hotel rooms?" I asked. "Or are the Swiss against that too?"

He gazed at me. A calm, clear gaze. "I'll come back with you."

"For the whole night?"

"Yes. The whole night."

As Arnold paid the bill and we walked out into the

rain, I felt a strange sense of grief—as though this were both the beginning and the end of our relationship. We walked the few blocks to the hotel and traveled upward in a tiny elevator. My room was small and rather elegant, with a double bed, a bureau, and a writing desk. The bathroom was huge. "Do you mind if I take a bath?" I said to Arnold. "I feel like I've been on the road for ten years."

"It's the change in time. It's nine o'clock here, but three in the afternoon back home."

The bathtub was deep and narrow, made of pink porcelain. I ran the water and poured in a packet of bubble bath. "Are Swiss bathrooms always so nice?" I called through the door.

"Always!" Arnold called back. "They have a thing about cleanliness."

I leaned back in the hot water and felt myself relaxing for the first time in days. It was three in the afternoon on Long Island, but here it was nine at night. I was in Zurich and Arnold Bromberg was with me. So fantastic, when you thought about it. So incredible. As though I had walked through a looking glass, like Alice.

I stepped out of the tub and dried myself with a pink bath towel. Then I slipped into my new nightgown. It was odd that I felt no sense of urgency, but now that Arnold and I were together, my sense of time was different.

When I emerged from the bathroom, Arnold was sitting on the side of the bed reading a magazine. He was fully clothed.

Not knowing how to proceed, I stood in the doorway. "I had a nice bath," I said. "It was wonderful."

He rose to his feet, and came over to me—and we looked at each other. "You're so tall," I said. "I had forgotten how tall."

At last we were kissing each other, and touching each other, and the world was slipping away. Both worlds were slipping away, the past and the present, Europe and America, and all of the problems of all the months we had been apart. Arnold took his clothes off one by one, letting them fall to the floor. Then he unbuttoned my nightgown and that fell to the floor too. Standing there in the middle of the room, we held each other and kissed. Slowly. Gently.

Arnold led me to the bed and pulled me down on top of him. I kissed him over and over, and the taste was salty. "You taste like the sea," I murmured. "The ocean."

He was leaning over me now, looking down at me, kissing my neck and my hair. Kissing my breasts. "There hasn't been anyone else," he said. "No one."

I knew that we could not wait any longer, and so I let him enter me, and for some reason I was crying again. "I love you," I said to him. "I always will."

Then, somewhere in the midst of this s
hurricane, I fell asleep.

21

I WOKE AT DAWN with Arnold's head on my breast.
A thin gray light was creeping through the window
and, as always, there were church bells ringing. "Arnold," I said, "I'm supposed to go home today."

Instantly, he was awake—sitting up in the bed,
running his hands through his hair, shaking the sleep
from his eyes. "What time is the plane?" he asked.

"Eleven o'clock. Can I change the reservation? Can
you do that?"

"Do you want to change it?"

"Yes, Arnold. Of course."

Arnold got out of bed, pulled on his shirt and trousers, and went into the bathroom. When he emerged,
he picked up the phone and, in German, asked the
operator to connect him to Swissair. When he got
through to them, he canceled my reservation. "I told
them that it was an emergency," he said. "That you'd
make another reservation in a few days."

"Well, it's the truth. This is an emergency. Our
being together, I mean."

oss the bed and kissed me. "Do you
one downstairs for breakfast?"
arving."

I watched Arnold with interest as he
phone and ordered two breakfasts. "How
did you learn so much German?" I asked.

"I studied it in college," he replied. "And it's all coming back."

"Can you speak Swiss-German too? The dialect?"

"A little. Enough to get by."

Fifteen minutes later there was a knock on the door—the person delivering our breakfasts. Feeling shy, I pulled the covers around me, but Arnold took the tray in the hall. *"Danke,"* he said to the maid.

We had our breakfast sitting at the little desk, and it was possibly the best breakfast of my life. Coffee with milk, and fresh rolls with butter and jam, and also some thick rye bread. Little packets of cheese. Ham too, sliced thinly. It was beautiful.

"Do I look fat?" I asked Arnold. "I've gained so much back again."

He took a swallow of coffee. "I've told you, darling, you look beautiful. We'll talk about your weight later."

After breakfast, Arnold took a shower—and we made love again. Slow, sensuous love, the hours ticking away, no sense of time, just the two of us and our bodies, which had always been perfect together. Arnold slept for a while, and then got up and had a cigaret. "You haven't stopped smoking," I said.

"I know. I tried, but I couldn't."

I sat on the edge of the bed, naked, but not feeling fat anymore. Feeling—if you can believe this—beautiful. Then I realized something important. The way I felt now, this moment, with Arnold, was the way all those housewives who read romances wanted to feel. Loved. Treasured. Valued. *Valued* was the word I had been searching for that night when my mother wept over *Wuthering Heights*. Women wanted to be valued.

"Arnold," I said, "do you value me?"

He looked surprised. "Totally," he said.

"Then why did you leave me? Not even a letter. Just a few words taped to the refrigerator."

"I can't go over it all again, Rita. I just can't."

"But how could you have done it?"

He ground out his cigaret in the ashtray. "Because I am twice your age, my darling, and because your parents were right. I have never earned a living. I am at heart a scholar."

"But what about the advance on your book?"

"My love, that was a small sum—and very few men could live on it. *I* am living on it because I am frugal."

"Arnold, we have to get married."

147

"You're not of age," he said. "We've gone over it a hundred times."

Realizing that this discussion was about to spoil everything, I decided to change course. "What should we do today? Would you show me the sights?"

"Of course, darling. What do you want to see?"

I came over and sat on his lap, still naked, and still feeling beautiful. "Everything. All the churches and all the museums. The zoo. The university."

He kissed me. "All right. I'll give you a guided tour."

"God!" I said suddenly. "Corry! She's meeting me at Kennedy airport today. What should I do?"

"Don't worry," said Arnold with his newfound sophistication. "We'll just give her a call."

As we dressed, Arnold explained to me that the best place to make phone calls was the railway station. Phoning from the hotel was exorbitant. We took the little elevator down to the lobby, and as we headed for the front doors no one even raised an eyebrow. Hotels, I decided, were wonderfully anonymous.

The sky was still gray, but the weather had lifted a little and it wasn't so humid. Arm in arm, Arnold and I strolled past a place called Bellevue, where there were a lot of streetcars, and then past the Odeon Cafe, where James Joyce had written part of *Ulysses*. "He's buried up near the zoo," Arnold said thoughtfully. "It's amazing."

"Who?" I said. "Ulysses?"

"No!" said Arnold. "James Joyce!" And we both started to laugh.

We crossed a bridge called the Quaibrucke, and stopped midway to look down at the river. We passed an open market, with people selling fruits and vegetables, and then we were on the Bahnhofstrasse. "It looks just like the pictures in my books!" I said. "It's gorgeous."

It was very simple to phone Corry. We entered a large room in the railway station that was filled with phone booths, and were assigned a booth by a man at a desk. Three minutes to New York would cost ten francs.

Dear God, I prayed, please let her be home. And as though God were listening, Corry picked up the phone. "It's me," I said. "It's me."

"Rita! Are you back already? I was asleep. What happened? Did everything go as planned?"

"Slow down," I said to her. "God, it's amazing. You sound like you're just around the corner."

"But where *are* you?"

"In Zurich. I didn't take the plane. I'm staying for a few more days."

"Oh no," she groaned.

"I can't help it. I need more time here. I still love him terribly, and he loves me. Nothing has changed."

"Then you found him on the Utoquai."

"Yes. Of course."

"Did you go to bed with him?" Corry asked.

"What do *you* think? Now, listen. I want you to phone my mother and tell her I've got the flu and laryngitis, and that I can't come home for a few days. Tell her I've got a fever."

"But it's August. People don't get the flu in August."

"Yes, they do."

"But suppose she doesn't believe me?"

"She will, she will," I said patiently.

"My parents are due home tonight, you know. Suppose your mother calls here and gets one of them?"

"Man the telephones," I said. "Don't let them answer. Anything, but just give me these few extra days."

"Well, OK," she said at last. "But it's risky. Listen, bring me a souvenir or something. All right?"

"You've got it. I'll bring you something wonderful."

For the rest of the day, Arnold and I explored Zurich. The zoo, and James Joyce's grave, and the university, and the National Museum. We climbed the narrow streets of the Old Town and took in a view of the city from a high square called the Lindenhof. We had sausages and beer in a crowded restaurant on the Bahnhofstrasse—and then we bought a present for Corry, a beautiful paisley scarf. The adults in Zurich looked very much like the ones back ho␣ the kids were wild. Punk haircuts dyed purple ␣ red, and black leather pants, and rouged cheeks. They stood on street corners handing out political leaflets. They lay on park benches, stoned.

As a hazy twilight drifted over the city, Arnold and I wound up at the Odeon Cafe, where I had coffee and he had a glass of red wine. It was just like a picture in one of my books at home—marble tables and potted palms, crystal chandeliers. I tried to imagine James Joyce sitting here, writing his masterpiece. I wondered if he had used a pencil or pen.

Arnold was lounging in his chair, smoking a long black cigaret. His hair was very bushy, very curly, and there was color in his cheeks. He wore no tie. I studied him and tried to understand how he could have changed so much in seven months. I mean, he was still the same person, but he seemed so sure of himself that it constantly surprised me. He spoke German like a native and knew all the local codes and manners. He paid for things easily, like he understood the money. Right now, he had taken a German newspaper from a wooden rack and was perusing it. Except for his sneakers, he could have been a Zuricher. Or, as he corrected me later, he could have been *Zurichoise*.

Who are you? I wondered. That shy, innocent man I met in Sag Harbor a year ago—or some kind of sophisticated traveler? You're so different now, Ar-

don't even know how to describe it to
almost . . . glamorous.

me over the city, and once more the bells
once more we went to dinner at the local
stubli. As we held hands across the table and stared at
one another, I realized, with a pain in my heart, that
Arnold had not yet said, "I love you." There was love
in his voice, and love in all his actions, but the words
were unspoken.

That night we made love for many hours—perfect,
beautiful love. The kind of love that all the housewives
of America were looking for, the kind of love that
made them turn to books. But for me, Rita Formica,
the love was real. As tangible as the salty taste of
Arnold's mouth, as true as his gentle hands on my
body. We made love and slept, woke and embraced
each other. And the night went on and on.

I woke at dawn to see him standing by the window
of the hotel room. Outside, along the lake, traffic was
already heading into the city. A door slammed down
the street and someone pulled a wooden cart along
the pavement—its wheels making a hollow sound. I
was not a city person, but I loved these noises. And
I loved the sight of Arnold, standing in his trousers
and shirt, barefoot. "I'm awake," I said to him.

He came over and sat on the edge of the bed. "You're
beautiful when you sleep. I've been watching you."

"Is it raining?"

"A little, but it's less humid today. We'll go over to the Fraumunster this morning. I want you to hear the organ."

I took his hand. "You've . . . changed so much, Arnold. Since you left America."

"Have I, darling? How?"

"I don't know. I don't have words for it."

He bent down and kissed me, and my eyes filled with tears. I can't explain it to you, but there was something about Arnold that always made me cry.

22

A FEW HOURS LATER we were walking into the Fraumunster cathedral. It was empty and silent, and our footsteps echoed on the vast floors. Holding my hand, Arnold led me over to the five stained-glass windows by Chagall. As I looked up at them, the sun broke through the gloomy weather and the windows shone. They were very tall and narrow, swimming with color, and I had never seen anything like them. Unable to speak, I squeezed Arnold's hand.

We sat down in one of the pews, and at exactly nine o'clock, Herr Kubli began to play the organ. I could not see the organ from where I sat, but Arnold had been right. It was like no other sound in the world. Herr Kubli was playing Bach, and the music swelled and grew until it filled the entire church.

Arnold's eyes were closed, and his whole body was responding to the music. I thought of the first time he had played the organ for me—in the Whalers Church in Sag Harbor—and how stunned I had been at his talent. But Herr Kubli played even better than Arnold. Herr Kubli was a genius.

And now the entire church seemed to be made of music, as Herr Kubli played Handel and Buxtehude. I knew the pieces he was playing because Arnold had educated me about organ music long ago. Long ago in another world on Long Island.

Herr Kubli practiced for an hour. When the concert was over, Arnold bowed his head silently, as though thanking Herr Kubli, and also thanking Bach and Handel. I could see why he came here every morning. I understood it.

We had brunch at a wonderful place called Sprungli, on the Bahnhofstrasse, and then—as sunlight took the place of gloom—we walked along the far side of the lake. Everyone in Zurich owned a dog, I decided, and all of the dogs were trained. Leashless, they trotted at their masters' sides. I thought of Mortimer, our dog at home, and felt a wave of sadness.

Arnold and I strolled around the lake and stood gazing at a huge stone lion that sat out in the water, on a pedestal. Lake Zurich was crowded with sail-boats, rowboats, and small excursion liners. "Would you like to take a boat trip today?" Arnold asked.

"No," I said, "let's just buy some snacks and picnic here. Near the lion."

Arnold went off to a nearby kiosk for crackers and juice, and two apples, and we picnicked on the grass by the lake. Lighting a cigaret, he stretched out with his head in my lap. All around us there were couples doing the same thing, stretching out together, kiss-ing, holding hands. "You said that the Swiss were puritanical," I said to Arnold, "but everyone *I* see around here looks sexy. Are these people puritans or not?"

"They are both, darling—both libertine and puri-tanical—and that's what makes them interesting. We'll go to the Niederdorf tonight, the bohemian quarter, and you'll see what I mean."

Buying me a new blouse to go with my blue jeans, and dressing up a little himself, Arnold guided me into the Niederdorf just after dusk. It was a maze of narrow winding streets near the Grossmunster, and it was a surprise.

Surprise is not the word. What the Niederdorf was, was a shock. Because, let me tell you, I had been unprepared for this. For the prostitutes and gay men with bleached hair, for the kids smoking dope right out in the open, and for the general air of decadence that pervaded the place. Bars, movie houses, and porno shops. Kids playing electric guitars. Couples necking in doorways. Girls with see-through blouses.

Arnold and I wandered into a bar called The Flamingo, and I was amazed. Not by the people, though they were very weird, but by Arnold. Arnold Bromberg in a low-down bar? Arnold drinking? I had always read that travel was broadening, but this was something different. When I had met him, Arnold had been innocent and fey, and as unworldly as a small-town minister. Now he was drinking scotch and chatting with the bartender, whom he knew, and whose name was Otto. "Crowded this evening, isn't it?" he said to Otto. *"Ja, ja,"* Otto replied. "The tourists, they are numerous tonight."

I sat there, perched on my barstool, drinking a Coke and feeling more and more uncomfortable. I wondered what Arnold's mother would say if she could see him in this joint.

"Look at the types," Arnold said to me under his breath. "They're interesting."

Interesting? The people at the bar were either men dressed like women, or women dressed like men, or a little of both. One man had on a red wig. Another had a poodle on his lap, and both the poodle and the man were wearing rhinestone chokers. "You're shocked," Arnold said to me. "I shouldn't have brought you here."

156

"No," I replied, "I'm glad you did. Bec
a part of Zurich, isn't it?"

"Yes," he said thoughtfully. "It's all a p
rich."

"I should really read up on this country," I said,
wanting to tease him. "I mean, I thought it was just
cows and yodeling. Chocolate bars."

Arnold laughed and pulled me close to him. "You're
wonderful," he said.

23

ON TUESDAY AFTERNOON, Arnold and I lay in bed together. It was raining again, I was tired from sight-
seeing, and there was very little time left. I had made
a reservation on Swissair for Wednesday morning,
and Corry, when I phoned her, said that my mother
had accepted the story of my flu. "Oh yes," my mother
had said, "Rita always seems to get those summer
viruses. Isn't it a shame?"

Arnold thought I was dozing, but I wasn't. I was
watching him out of the corner of my eye. He had
been restless all day, and in between times of lovemaking would get up and pace the room and smoke.
I had not yet broached the topic that was uppermost

, mind, but I knew I had to do it now. Tomorrow
,orning, I would be gone. "Arnold?" I said tentatively. He was standing by the window, looking out
at the traffic.

"It's amazing how people drive here," he said. "A
hundred miles an hour, then they screech to a halt at
a stoplight. Yes, darling? What's on your mind?"

Us, I wanted to say. Us, and getting married, and
living together for the rest of our lives. Us, Arnold,
us. "Uh, nothing too drastic," I said. "I was just
wondering if you'd miss Zurich when you come
home."

"Miss it?" he said vaguely.

"Yes, Arnold. When you come back home. To Sag
Harbor."

He gave me a strange look. "But Rita, I'm not
going back to Sag Harbor. Whatever made you think
that?"

A hand of fear clutched at my heart, and then it
went away. "Well, maybe not Sag Harbor. I mean,
maybe that's not the right place for us. But you *will*
be coming back to America, won't you?"

"No," he said, "actually, I won't. I'm staying here."

I felt as if all the blood had been drained from my
body, but you wouldn't have known it from my voice.
"I don't get it," I said. "I mean, you can't stay here
forever, can you?"

He sat down at the little desk and stubbed out his

cigaret. "I shall stay as long as my money lasts. I want to finish the book here. I want to work with Herr Kubli."

"Work with him?"

Arnold looked sheepish. "I haven't told you this yet, but Herr Kubli has agreed to take me on as a pupil. At the Fraumunster. I played for him the other day, just before you arrived, and he seemed to think I had promise."

Promise? I thought. *Promise?* Arnold, you're thirty-three years old!

I tried to keep my voice steady, but it was already starting to break. "But what about us? The two of us? Our future?"

"We have no future," said Arnold Bromberg. "Nothing has changed."

"What do you mean, nothing has changed? I've come all the way over here. I've . . ."

"Yes," said Arnold, "and when you return home, I will still be a man twice your age, who cannot support you, and your parents will feel just as they felt last year."

I got out of bed and pulled a blouse on over my nakedness. Then I went over to Arnold and sat down at the little desk. "The thing that has changed is us. *We* are different, and next summer I'll be eighteen."

"You have college ahead of you."

"To hell with college. Arnold! What's the matter with you? Don't you care about us at all?"

"I care!" he said angrily. "But nothing has changed, Rita."

I was crying now, softly and hopelessly, sitting at the little desk. "Then why did you let all this happen? Why did you make love to me? We've been making love for days."

"I didn't ask you to come over here!"

"And yet you let everything start up again."

"Because I care for you."

"If you did, you would marry me."

"God!" he exploded. "You are so young, so young. You think that everything can be solved by marriage. Well, let me tell you something. Men who get into their thirties without marrying probably never will. I'm just not marriage material, as your mother would say. And you must go to college."

"No," I said coldly, "I mustn't. Because, Arnold Bromberg, there are no two people on earth more right for each other than you and me. And if we blow it now, we may never have another chance for happiness. There aren't too many chances in life, so when a person is given one he should take it."

"I must finish my book. I must study with Herr Kubli."

I stood in front of him and took his face in my hands. "OK, if that's how you want it. Stay in this

160

weird place. Finish your book. Study the organ. But I won't let you go. I'll be back there on Long Island, far away, on the other side of an ocean, but I'll be with you every moment. Look me in the eye and tell me that you don't want to spend the rest of your life with me. Go on, do it!"

"We've said enough," Arnold said quietly. "Let's get dressed, Rita. Let's go for a walk."

So we went for a walk, and had one last, sad, final dinner at the little *stubli* around the corner—but it wasn't the same. The argument we had had stood between us like a barrier, a wall.

That night, Arnold left me in front of my hotel. "Would you like me to take you to the airport tomorrow?" he asked.

I shook my head. "That won't be necessary, Arnold. Actually, I'd rather go alone."

"There's a bus to the airport, you know. The hotel clerk will tell you about it."

"No problem. Well, so long now. It's been fun."

"Will you write to me, Rita?"

"I don't know."

Pain came into his eyes, and he reached out for my hand. "Don't sound like that."

"So how should I sound? Like a Woody Allen movie? Good-bye now, Arnold, good-bye."

He was still holding my hand. "This isn't the end."

"What would you call it? The beginning?"

"Don't be bitter."

"Bitter? I'm not bitter. I've just aged a hundred years, that's all, a hundred years in four days. A good trick, if you can do it. So good-bye and good luck."

He did a strange thing then. Which was that he put his arms around me and buried his face in my neck. Like a little boy. It was such a sincere gesture—and so sad—that for one moment I wanted to take back everything I had said. I just wanted to hold him in my arms, and stay in Zurich, and become a Swiss housewife. And if he didn't want to marry me, then I would be his mistress, or lover, or whatever he wanted to call it.

"I'll tell you something," I said, "and I want you to listen to this very carefully, because it's the truth. Our problem isn't my age, or your income. And our problem isn't my parents, either. Our problem is simply that you're a confirmed bachelor, Arnold Bromberg, who is scared as hell of responsibility. You pursued Rose because she was unavailable, and you pursued me because I was too young, and the next woman you love will probably be all wrong too. However. When you get over this childishness, I, Rita, will be waiting for you in Sag Harbor. *Aufwiedersehen.*"

Arnold's mouth had dropped open in surprise. But he didn't have time to speak, because by the time he had collected himself I was in the elevator, going up

162

to my room. I wanted to take a hot bath, and pack, and have an early night. Because the plane left at eleven.

24

THIS TIME MY seat on Swissair was by the window, and my neighbor was not into Dainty Dolly hairbrushes. My neighbor, in fact, was an Asian man who did not speak to me at all, so I had plenty of time to stare out the window and plan my re-entry into the United States. I ordered a glass of white wine and Chicken Marengo for lunch. I watched the movie, which was a thriller starring Dustin Hoffman.

Either I was paralyzed emotionally or I had just died without knowing it, because I felt absolutely nothing. On the other hand, it is possible for a Wall Street tycoon who has been wiped out to feel nothing too—and for a man who is facing a firing squad to be pleasant and calm. Equanimity is no proof of anything.

My whole life had just collapsed, and there I was, sipping a glass of white wine. Watching a movie.

Arnold valued me, but did not want to marry me.

He made me feel loved when we were together, but didn't really want me. Fantastic, said one of those inner voices I was always hearing—and also terrible. But not irrevocable. The point is, Rita Formica, what are you going to do now?

Write a romance, said another voice. A real one. The story of me and Arnold Bromberg.

I stared at the man who was sitting next to me, but I wasn't seeing him at all. Because what I was seeing was an entire book, a *real* romance, that told the story of Arnold and me. God! I even had the title. And the chapters would be around thirty pages each. And the man would be a painter instead of a writer, but the girl would definitely be me. Short, fat, and desperate.

That was the trouble, said yet another voice. You were *too* desperate, too needy. And you depended on Arnold to make you thin. The only person who can make you thin, kiddo, is you.

I would call the book *All the Slow Dances*, in honor of the fact that Arnold had once confessed to me that he could only dance to slow music, old-fashioned tunes like "My Funny Valentine." But the slow music would mean other things too. Symbolic things.

Suddenly, I was overwhelmed with the desire to write. Flooded with it. Because somewhere deep inside of me I knew that writing could save me right now—redeem me, even. I whipped a pad and pencil out of my purse and began.

The flight home went quickly, and we arrived at Kennedy at three in the afternoon, New York time. Corry had wanted to meet me at the airport, but I had asked her not to. I wanted to take the bus back to Long Island in peace.

Five days. I had been away for five days, and yet the person who sat on that bus, speeding down to the east end of Long Island, was not Rita Formica at all. I had left for Europe as one kind of female, and was returning home as another. Fantastic.

As the bus rattled along the expressway, I closed my eyes and thought about men. Men who just wanted sex, like Jerry, and men who were romantics, like Arnold—but who didn't want to get trapped—and then I thought about men like my father, who get married and support families and wind up drinking too much. For one moment, Arnold's face appeared before me—sweet, intelligent, distinguished—and then I put him out of my mind. There would be time to think about Arnold, and miss Arnold, but that time wasn't now. . . . Oh, God. There was the exit to the Hamptons, exit 70. Then the Sunrise Highway, and after that good old Route 27. The bus made its way through Water Mill and Bridgehampton. People got off, and new people got on. It was early September, and in one week school would be starting. As the bus pulled into Sag Harbor, four swans flew over the North Haven bridge.

Feeling very odd, I got off the bus and stood on Main Street. The Heavenly Cafe was crowded with people about to have dinner. Housewives were coming out of the IFA grocery store with packages in their arms. How tiny everything looked, and how nice— the Municipal Building with its white cupola, the hotel with its old-fashioned façade.

I walked the few blocks home, marveling at how small everything looked, how American. And when I approached my house I saw that Mortimer, our dog, was sleeping in the front yard. He did not wake as I passed him and went up the front steps. Crazily enough, my mother was standing at the stove, looking like she hadn't budged for five days. She was wearing the same blue apron, and she was even stirring something that needed more salt. "Rita?" she said, as I walked into the kitchen. "Is that you, sweetie? How's your flu bug?"

"Gone," I said. "Forever cured."

My mother turned and looked me over. Then she went back to stirring whatever was in the pot. "Did you have a nice time with Corry? Did you do anything special?"

"Nothing much. We just fooled around."

"I feel that you've been so far away," she said. "It's silly, but that's how I feel."

I went over and kissed her on the back of the neck, like I always do. "What's for dinner, Mama Mia? I'm starving to death."

"Veal," she said, "a lovely new recipe for veal stew. And do you know what's on television tonight?" She laughed self-consciously. *"Wuthering Heights!"*

'Easy to pick up, hard to put down'

C. S. Adler
Binding Ties

Anne's life is dominated by her mother and grandmother, and a passionate affair with Kyle offers the chance of escape – but for how long?

Judy Blume
Forever

Catherine and Michael's relationship seems to be forever. But will love last when they are separated?

Bruce Brooks
The Moves Make the Man

Nothing fazes Jerome Fox, not even crossing the road to become the first black student at Wilmington School. But he can't make out Bix Rivers – the sharpest white guy he has ever seen.

Aidan Chambers
Dance on my Grave

From beginning to end it was a dangerous dream which lasted seven weeks. Exactly 49 days. Now the court is demanding some kind of explanation . . .

Lois Duncan
The Eyes of Karen Connors

She can see things that no one else can see. She *knows* things she can't possibly know. Where is her power coming from?

I Know What You Did Last Summer

Somebody knows what really happened that night . . . and they'll go to any lengths to get revenge.

Stranger with my Face

Was she going crazy? Or was something really horribly sinister casting a shadow across her life?

Paula Fox
The Moonlight Man

Catherine's quiet and peaceful life is exposed to the mysterious influence of the Moonlight Man.

Merrill Joan Gerber
Also Known as Sadzia! The Belly Dancer

Sandy's fed up with her mother's comments about her size, so she agrees to exercise: with one very strange condition!

I'm Kissing as Fast as I Can

Sid's father is all for encouraging his son's love life, but Sid is looking for true love.

Virginia Hamilton
A Little Love

The car wasn't up to much. But they had the rest of their lives to make the journey of discovery.

Toeckey Jones
Skin Deep

Everything was against them. The country, the time . . . and the colour of his skin.

M. E. Kerr
If I Love You, am I Trapped Forever?

Alan Bennett is cool – or so he thinks. And he just can't understand it when someone else gets all the attention.

Is That You, Miss Blue?

Flanders Brown reckoned she was pretty unconventional. But she was no match for the teacher with a direct line through to Jesus.

Night Kites

The night of the Springsteen concert was a night for revelations . . . and the start of some lessons in love . . .

Norma Klein
Angel Face

As the only one still left at home, guess who ended up looking after everything?

Beginner's Love

Joel and Leda happily shared so many first times together. But when things go wrong Leda is on her own.

Breaking Up

Now she's back with her father, and her mother's fallen in love with another woman, Alison isn't sure about anything, except her feelings for Ethan.

Going Backwards

He'd waited all this time for a chance to grow up. Now everyone around him was growing old . . .

It's Not What you Expect

When the drama was over Carla couldn't imagine things ever being the same again. But maybe they had never been the way she imagined them in the first place . . .

All Pan books are available at your local bookshop or newsagent, or can be ordered direct from the publisher. Indicate the number of copies required and fill in the form below.

Send to: **CS Department, Pan Books Ltd., P.O. Box 40, Basingstoke, Hants. RG21 2YT.**

or phone: 0256 469551 (Ansaphone), quoting title, author and Credit Card number.

Please enclose a remittance* to the value of the cover price plus: 60p for the first book plus 30p per copy for each additional book ordered to a maximum charge of £2.40 to cover postage and packing.

*Payment may be made in sterling by UK personal cheque, postal order, sterling draft or international money order, made payable to Pan Books Ltd.

Alternatively by Barclaycard/Access:

Card No.

Signature:

Applicable only in the UK and Republic of Ireland.

While every effort is made to keep prices low, it is sometimes necessary to increase prices at short notice. Pan Books reserve the right to show on covers and charge new retail prices which may differ from those advertised in the text or elsewhere.

NAME AND ADDRESS IN BLOCK LETTERS PLEASE:

Name —

Address —

3/87